Dandelion Dreams

Penny Harmon

Table of Contents

Chapter One

Maddie Jones hung up the phone and dropped to the floor. Nothing could have prepared her for what she just heard. Her Aunt Daisy was dead. The shocking part was not that she was dead—it was the fact that Maddie thought she had been dead for twenty-years.

Her mother had been the one to break the news to her when she was nine-years-old. She had sat her down on her bed and leaned in closer to say, "I am so sorry, Madelyn, but Aunt Daisy is gone."

"What do you mean? Gone?" young Maddie asked.

Her mother looked away to the window. "She died. I'm so sorry you won't be able to see her again."

Maddie had cried her heart out that day and vowed to remember her favorite aunt forever. She kept a picture of her aunt on her desk and, whenever she was feeling a little down, she would talk to her. Twenty years later she still did it. Broken heart? Talk to Aunt Daisy. Not sure why you didn't get a pay raise? Talk it over with Aunt Daisy.

And whenever someone told her she reminded them of Daisy, she held her head up high. Daisy had been known as the black sheep of the family, although her aunt had once told her, "I'm more of a gray sheep." Maddie laughed at the memory.

For twenty-years, she thought her aunt was dead. What had her mother been thinking? Her father? He must have known, too. That story had to have been something her mother and her family concocted. A scheme so none of them would be embarrassed by Daisy's actions again. Unfortunately, both were now gone, and she had no way to find out what really happened to Aunt Daisy twenty years ago.

Taking a deep breath, Maddie picked herself up off the floor. She had things to do. The attorney she had spoken with said it was imperative she come to Maine immediately to accept or decline her inheritance. Decline? Why would somebody even think about turning down an inheritance?

She would have to take some time off work. The ad agency she worked for was one of the largest in Boston, and she had worked hard to earn her position in the company. She heard she was up for a promotion soon. She did not want to jeopardize her job. After all, Wendy was not exactly easy to work for most of the time and could hold a grudge like nobody else. But what was she supposed to do?

After getting her suitcase out of the closet, she sat down on the stool at the kitchen counter and picked up her phone. As she dialed her best friend, Kyra, she thought back to the call to her boss. Wendy had told her to take all the time she needed and to check in when she returned to Boston. Of course, she had said it in her most patronizing voice. Maddie could not imagine what she would be like when she returned.

When Kyra answered the phone, Maddie got right to the point. "My Aunt Daisy died and left me an inheritance. The lawyer said she just died, but I was told she died twenty years ago. I don't understand what's going on and now I have to go to Maine and…"

Kyra interrupted. "Slow down. I have no idea what you are talking about. I remember when your aunt died. We were in fourth grade."

Taking a deep breath, Maddie continued. "I know. I don't get it. My parents told me my aunt died twenty years ago, but now a lawyer calls me up and tells me she just died."

After a short pause, Kyra stated, "That doesn't make any sense at all. Who else in your family can you ask about it?"

"My mother's brother, who would have been Daisy's brother, too, died last year of cancer. That's all there was…the three of them. I doubt anyone on my father's side would know anything, but I will call my Aunt Evie."

"When are you going to Maine? What did she leave you?" Kyra asked. "Do you want me to go with you?"

"I wish you could, but I'm leaving in the morning. Wendy isn't happy about it, but what am I supposed to do? I have to go. I don't know what she left me, but the lawyer said I have to be there to accept it or decline it."

"I can't imagine why they would say you could decline it. I wonder what it is. What if it's a business? You could be your own boss, Maddie!"

"I doubt it. The last time I saw Aunt Daisy, she had a farm on the coast in the middle of nowhere. Can you imagine me living in the country?" While Maddie had loved visiting as a child, she could not imagine it now. Dirt? Bugs? Animals? Definitely not her thing. And she preferred her *Jimmy Choos* over Muck boots.

Kyra's laughter took over the airwaves and Maddie could not help but grin. They had tried camping. Once. That was enough for either of them.

"Well, even if she left you the farm, you could sell it and pretty much do what you want with the money. Or maybe she left you money instead? Then you wouldn't have to worry about the hassle of it all."

Maddie had thought about all that, too. She would feel bad selling her aunt's farm if it was what she inherited. But she could not imagine living anywhere but the city—in her apartment with the perfect location. The last twelve years, Boston had been her home and, really, the only place she felt comfortable.

"I'll call you tomorrow night and let you know what's going on. I'll probably be back tomorrow night anyway."

After hanging up the phone, Maddie quickly packed her bag with enough items to get her through the weekend in case she did decide to stay for more than one night. She also threw in a bathing suit. Her aunt's farm was right on the coast and the private beach was only a five-minute walk from the farmhouse. It was always one of her favorite things about visiting the farm. Of course, her aunt always called it a farm, but it was nothing more than a large farmhouse in the middle of a field. She did have a few laying hens, but that was it. Farm? Not quite. But she did wonder if the little town her aunt lived in had been transformed into something larger.

***

Driving to Cove's Port Maddie's stomach churned. It had been twenty years since she had been to Maine. It had always seemed so far away when she was a child. As the Welcome to Maine sign came into view, she glanced at the clock on her dashboard. Less than two hours. It would be another hour to get to Cove's Port, causing Maddie to wince. All this time her aunt had been three hours away. If only she had known.

While there was a stoplight in the middle of Main Street in Cove's Port, nothing else looked like it had changed much. Even the ice cream parlor where she and her aunt used to go still stood on the corner of Main and Elm. Although it could use a paint job, the signs were still boasting the largest ice cream cones on the coast. It was the quintessential small town.

Before she had left Boston, she looked up the town on the Internet and found twelve-hundred people called Cove's Port their home year-round. There were several seasonal cottages near the beaches, which were rented out in the summer, but for the most part, the town was not a tourist attraction. Boothbay Harbor, a half-hour to the south, and Camden, an hour north, seemed to attract more tourists.

She had not thought coming back would cause a lot of emotion, but she was suddenly drowning in memories of happier times. She did not come to her aunt's house as often as she wanted to, but when she did it was usually during her week-long vacation from school or when school let out in the summer. She and her older sister, Phoenix, would take turns. Sadly, she had never gotten her last summer visit with Aunt Daisy because Phoenix had gone when school got out and, after a call home to ask her parents, was allowed to stay until school was ready to begin.

Oh, she had been mad about that. Her mother and father explained that being sixteen, Phoenix needed a break before she entered her junior year of high school. And it would keep her away from her boyfriend for a few months. That was a bonus for her parents. They said they did not want Phoenix getting too serious with any boy. At nine-years-old, her needs did not matter. Or that was how she felt.

After being told her Aunt Daisy had died a week after her sister returned home, Maddie did what any nine-year-old would do. She had blamed her sister. For the next two years, she barely spoken to her, but that was her biggest regret and a whole different story.

When a truck pulled into the parking space beside her, Maddie's thoughts were interrupted. A glance at the clock on her dash revealed she had about fifteen minutes before she was to meet with the lawyer. Grabbing her purse and keys, she got out of her Toyota Camry and locked the doors. Not really needed around this town, but it was a habit she had learned quickly in the city.

Walking up the sidewalk, she went past the entrance of the hardware store and then the small coffee shop. In between an antique shop and a used bookstore, she found his office. Turning back around, she walked the short distance to *The Grind* and opened the door.

She and her aunt had come in here a few times when she was a kid. Aunt Daisy did not go anywhere without a coffee in hand. Like her aunt, she also traveled with a coffee cup and figured after the almost three-hour ride, it was needed before she saw Mr. Bingham.

Inside, Maddie looked around and realized nothing looked the same at The Grind as it did twenty years ago. The black-and-white checkered floor had been replaced with what appeared to be laminated flooring and the old rickety booths were replaced with small, patio-sized tables for two.

At the counter, she ordered a large coffee with extra sugar and cream to go and took a step back. Her aunt's friend, Carol, had run the place when she was there the last time. Maybe she could get some information from her about her aunt.

"Excuse me?" she said to the cashier. "Does Carol still own this place?"

The cashier, who looked a few years older than she did, shook her head. "Lord, no. Carol sold this place to me about ten years ago and moved to Florida."

Figures, she thought. To the cashier, she replied, "Good for her… and you. I used to come here when I was a kid. Did you know Daisy Carr?"

"Oh yes, I knew Daisy. I'm so sad she's gone. Are you a relative?" she asked.

"I'm her niece. I'm sorry. I should have introduced myself. Maddie Jones." Maddie set her money on the counter and watched as the cashier smiled.

"It's nice to meet you, Maddie. Just sorry it's under these circumstances. I'm Delia Jackson. I take it you're here to see Sal?" Delia handed Maddie her change and stepped from behind the counter.

Throwing the change into the tip jar, Maddie nodded her head. "Yeah, just heading to his office now."

"Well, if you need anything…a cup of coffee…a shoulder… stop back in," Delia said.

"Thanks so much." That was what she remembered about Cove's Port. Everyone was friendly even if they did not know you. Boston was nothing like this place. The people who lived in Boston were friendly enough if they knew you, but the truth was everyone was too busy to pay attention to anyone else. At least it was like that where she lived and worked. It really was how she preferred it in her everyday life.

Grabbing her coffee, Maddie exited the coffee shop and walked back toward the lawyer's office. She still could not get over how quaint the town seemed. As a kid, she did not pay much attention to things like cobblestone, benches, or streetlights, but the way everything meshed gave her a feeling like she was coming home. The thought scared her, and she quickly hurried to her appointment.

***

"What do you mean? A boy?" Maddie's mouth hung open. Confusion seemed to be an understatement for this meeting.

The lawyer, who asked her to call him Sal, sat back in his chair. "Pardon me, a young man. Twenty years ago, Daisy adopted an infant. She never had children of her own and chose to adopt Kyle right after his birth. He now resides on Dandelion Farm, but he needs assistance. He is not able to completely care for himself. Your aunt's will states very clearly you must become his guardian to inherit the rest of her estate. If you choose not to accept your inheritance, the inheritance, including the money, will be passed onto the next person on the list and you will receive one dollar."

What? How could her aunt have adopted a child twenty-years ago? It must have happened right after Phoenix came back from Aunt Daisy's. Her sister had never said a word to her about it and, at sixteen, Phoenix had trouble keeping quiet about anything. She could not imagine Phoenix keeping anything a secret. None of this made sense.

To the lawyer, she said, "I don't get it. My parents told me Daisy died twenty years ago. Do you know anything about that?"

Sal shook his head. "I don't. I do know, however, your sister's name was first on the list, but when she died unexpectedly, Daisy came in and removed her name and placed you down as the first to inherit should something happen to her. Your parent's names were never on her list to be contacted."

"You don't know why?" she inquired. Something was not adding up.

Sal shrugged his shoulders. "There were rumors, but honestly, I don't want to say anything unless I know for certain. Why don't we take a ride out to Dandelion Farm and let you see for yourself what you have inherited? If you don't have any interest in it…well, I'd rather go right to the next name on the list."

"Can you tell me more about the boy Daisy adopted? You said he's unable to take care of himself?"

Sal leaned back in his chair. "Kyle is a great young man with Down Syndrome. Are you familiar with what it is?"

Maddie sighed and nodded. Yes, she was familiar with it. She and Kyra had helped coordinate a walk to raise money on World Down Syndrome Day a few years ago. She never thought Down Syndrome would have a direct impact on her own life, though.

"Kyle is high-functioning. He has a job, but he does not drive. Daisy was the one who usually took him back and forth to work. His social worker has since stepped in and has been caring for him and the farm. However, Lincoln has his job and cannot take care of the farm indefinitely. He has taken a leave of absence to take care of Kyle until this is sorted out. So, if you are willing to take your inheritance, you will need to move to Dandelion Farm as soon as possible to relieve him. On top of this, you will never have to worry about money again. Daisy knew how to manage her money and investments quite well. With the value of the property, her assets, and investments, it totals up to almost two million dollars."

Chapter Two

By the time she got into her car to follow Sal to the farm, Maddie's head was swimming. She was not even thirty. She did not know if she ever wanted children of her own, let alone take over the care for a young man with Down Syndrome. What the heck was her aunt thinking about when she chose her? And why the falling out between her and the family? With both her parents and her sister gone, and now Daisy, it was doubtful she would ever get the answers she wanted.

Maddie followed Sal down a familiar road running parallel to the ocean. She rolled down her window and breathed in the salty air. The smell brought back memories she thought forgotten. Before she knew it, Sal's car was signaling a turn after the view of the ocean disappeared. The first thing Maddie noticed was the large sign at the end of the drive stating Dandelion Farm. Underneath the sign, there was another advertising fresh eggs, fresh mozzarella cheese, and baby pigs. Oh Lord! What had Daisy done in the last twenty years? And now everything might be hers? Pigs? Chickens? And a special needs boy? Not exactly her dream. Her dream was back in Boston.

As she followed Sal's car down the long, dirt driveway, she noticed the fields on either side and smiled. Dandelions were in bloom, and they filled the fields with yellow. And there was a cow right out in the middle of it all. Shaking her head in disbelief, she could barely breathe as Sal's car stopped in front of the yellow farmhouse. She parked between his car and an old Subaru looking like it belonged in a junk yard.

Stepping out of the car, Maddie looked around and took note of all the changes. Where the small hen house had once been there was now a much larger and sturdier hen house. About a hundred feet back from the hen house sat a barn looking like it could house at least twenty cows. She cringed at the thought. So much had changed, and yet, it was the same.

Sal turned around and told her, "The farmhouse comes with forty acres and there is several hundred feet of shoreline included. There is also a private beach. Taxes are high because of the water frontage, but that happens in this area. Lately, we've had a lot of out-of-staters coming in to buy land." Pointing to the back of the property, Sal added, "Along with the farmhouse, there is the barn and a couple of other animal pens out back a little further. Daisy has pigs, but wanted to keep them away from the house, which believe me, is a smart thing, and you'll find out why."

While Sal continued to talk about what came with the inheritance, Maddie continued her visual inspection of the property. The house itself seemed solid, and Daisy's once small collection of wood scraps and metal was now triple the size of what it was when she had last been here.

"…and Lincoln has been taking care of it since your aunt died, so I'm sure he'll be happy to see you. Do you have any questions? I'm sure you'd like to explore, but you may want to change your shoes before you try that. Give this a chance, Maddie. If you accept this inheritance, you will not have to worry about money again and…well, you may just find yourself glad you did."

Looking down at her feet to see her white high heels, Maddie could only grin. "Yeah, I think I better change. As for the inheritance, I really need to think about it."

Sal opened his car door and Maddie must have looked at him with confusion, because he quickly added. "The door is unlocked, so make yourself comfortable. Lincoln is expecting you here today, so there won't be any surprise. I will see you in my office soon. Stop by anytime."

"You're leaving…you are leaving me here alone?" she stammered.

Sal let out a laugh. "You will be perfectly fine. You've been here before. The dogs are probably inside, but they're friendly, so no worries there."

"You can't stay?" she managed to ask in between swallows.

"I have another appointment. If anything comes up, just let me know. I think Lincoln and Kyle will be home around four. I'll see you soon." With that said, Sal got into his car, backed up, and drove back down the long drive leaving her standing by her car all by herself.

What was she supposed to do now? It was not like she was going to let herself in and make herself comfortable. Although, if she did accept the inheritance then all of this would be hers. Well, not really. According to the will, she would share it with Kyle, and she was not exactly sure how welcoming he would be.

Speaking of Kyle, why would her aunt adopt an infant with special needs? According to what she remembered about her aunt, she had always liked kids, but she had never wanted any of her own. What could have changed that? But, then again, people changed, and she was a child when she knew her aunt. Maybe she did not really know her at all? Either way, Maddie thought her aunt was crazy for adopting a child so late in her life.

Picking up her phone, Maddie checked messages and then realized it was only noon. Her stomach was rumbling, but there was no way she was going in the house by herself. Friendly dogs or not. Instead, she got back into her car and drove back to town.

***

In the local pizza shop, she ordered a ham Italian, grabbed a couple bottles of water, and then headed right back to the farm. She would have herself a little picnic down by the beach and, hopefully, when Kyle was brought home, she could figure everything out.

Stepping out of the vehicle, Maddie grabbed her purse and the bag holding her sandwich and drinks. She walked around the back of the house to find the path that would take her to the private beach. She was not exactly dressed for it, but it would beat sitting around waiting for someone to show up.

It wasn't until she passed by a small building and heard a hissing sound she realized her mistake. She should not have ventured off so far without first assessing the situation. The next thing she knew, two geese were in hot pursuit…of her. With a screech, she turned back toward the direction of the house and ran as fast as she could. Running on an uneven path with high heels was certainly not an easy feat. But it was either run or be attacked by those two large monstrosities. She was not having any of that.

By the time she made it around the corner of the house, the geese had backed off and were waddling back toward their own house. They were making a lot of noise and, if she did not know any better, laughing at her because their scare tactics won.

Deciding the front porch would have to do for now, Maddie walked up the steps and sat down at the top. So much had changed since the last time she had stepped foot on the farm. The last time she was at the farm, Aunt Daisy had two dogs. Bullet was an old hound dog who never left the porch. Tweedle-Dee had been an old sheepdog who followed Maddie everywhere she went.

The one-time Maddie had wandered too far away and could not find her way back, it was Tweedle-Dee who had rescued her. He barked and ran off into the woods only stopping to make sure she was following. Smiling at the memory, Maddie opened a bottle of water and took a gulp. Obviously, the two dogs were gone now. But there was no doubt in her mind Daisy had picked some unique dogs to replace them. She was not sure if she was ready to find out as she got up to open the old screen door.

***

Cautiously, she peeked in the window and then twisted the door handle. Maddie was thankful it was unlocked, but she was nervous about what she might find. The last thing she needed was to be attacked by a dog, especially after her confrontation with the belligerent geese. Pushing it open a few inches, she stuck her head in far enough to make sure it was clear. She called out, "Anybody here?"

A tiny bark from a room at the back of the house erupted and she could hear the pitter-patter of feet coming toward her. Preparing to shut the door quickly if need be, she laughed when around the corner came a tiny dog weighing no more than a pound or two. It was a Yorkshire Terrier, and with no fear, she opened the door wider. "Oh, look at you! You are adorable!" The dog sat down about three feet in front of her and proceeded to bark.

Maddie stepped in and shut the door behind her. It was not until she heard the sound of a yawn from the corner that she froze. Turning her head, her eyes landed on one of the biggest shepherds she had ever seen. He was lying on a dog bed. His ears pointed straight up, and his head cocked to the side, but he did not move. His muzzle all gray, she realized he was an old dog and did not want to bother getting up for someone who meant no harm. But she still did not dare to move.

"Well, hello big boy! You scared me with that big old yawn of yours. Don't worry, buddy. I'm not going to hurt you. I just thought I'd pop in and check on you. This was my Aunt Daisy's house." Realizing she was carrying on a conversation with a dog, she smiled. It had been too long since she had a dog in her life. While her aunt had loved animals, her parents had not.

"Animals bring dirt in the house. They're nasty," her mother would tell her. Maddie would roll her eyes until her mother scolded her.

Sitting down on the floor, confident the old dog would not lunge at her, she spoke softly. "What's your name? You look very regal. Is it Duke? Sargent? I know Aunt Daisy loved to pick just the right names for her babies."

The German Shepherd cocked his head to one side and let out a whine.

"You must miss her a lot." Scooting closer to the dog, she held out her hand. "Don't worry, I'm not going to hurt you."

She watched as the shepherd lifted his paw to her and she laughed. "You are a good boy, aren't you?" It was not long before he was resting his head in her lap. The Yorkie had since retreated and was nowhere in sight.

Looking around the large dining room, a sigh escaped from Maddie. It was like she was ten-years-old again and sitting on the floor with her aunt's old hound dog, Bullet. Anyone who heard the name associated it with a fast dog and one that did not sit still. Old Bullet was the opposite. He barely moved all day. Aunt Daisy thought the name Bullet might inspire him. She had been wrong. Bullet rarely got up, except to do his duty outside or to move closer to the food dish. Maddie had loved him regardless.

Of course, the dining room and the kitchen looked quite different than it had more than twenty years ago. The Formica countertop was now granite, and the cupboards had been updated to white. The floors, which had once been an ugly yellow vinyl were now hardwood. It would certainly look out of place in her apartment in Boston, but it was perfect for the old farmhouse.

After wiping her eyes, Maddie decided to do a little more investigating. She petted the shepherd on top of the head and stood up. Wandering from the kitchen to the next room, she startled once again as she found two dogs lying on the couch staring at her.

One, a Golden Retriever, wagged its tail, but like the shepherd, did not move from its position. The other, some type of Lab mix, closed its eyes, going back to sleep on the couch. Well, one thing was certain, her aunt's love for dogs remained. If anything, her aunt's love for animals had escalated. She looked around the room but did not see any more. With no fear of any of the dogs removing themselves from the couch, she surveyed the room.

Pictures of a young boy with wide eyes and a bright smile adorned the walls showcasing the various stages of his life. His straight, blondish-brown hair was cut short and his dimples reminded Maddie of her own. It was evident in every picture along the walls how much he was loved, and Maddie felt a slight pain of envy. He had been happy with her aunt, while she did not even know she was alive.

Shaking her head, Maddie knew it would not do any good to hold any resentment toward her cousin Kyle. She was not sure what his capabilities were, but she knew he held no fault for her belief that her aunt was dead. The last thing she wanted to do was start out their new relationship—if that was what you could call it—on a bad note.

Off to the left of the living room was the sunroom. As she stepped inside, her heart constricted quickly. Nothing in it had changed at all. While the kitchen and living room had been updated, the sunroom reflected all things of the past. The same daybed sat in the corner; the same one she had slept on so many years ago when the nights had been too hot to sleep upstairs.

The easel where she painted pictures of sunsets still stood in the corner. Just above it hung one of the paintings she had done when she had been about eight. The edges had curled, and the paint had faded, but it was still hanging on the wall right where she had left it. Wiping at a tear making its way down her cheek, a noise from behind her pulled her back to the present.

The little Yorkie who met her at the door was now standing in the doorway, and it let out a whine.

Taking a step closer to the dog, Maddie reached down to pick it up. When she did the little dog almost melted into her arms. Discovering the dog was a female, Maddie whispered, "What's the matter, girl?"

The Yorkie whined against Maddie's chest and she held her close. Noticing the tag on the pink collar, Maddie read the name, Peaches, and grinned. "Peaches, is it?" The little dog yipped and licked her chin.

"Hmm, Miss Peaches. I think I need to do a little more investigating." Walking back into the living room, she deposited Peaches onto the small chair by the fireplace and approached the two dogs lying on the couch. Leaning over to the Golden Retriever, she looked and found a tag with the name Bella on it. The Lab never batted an eye when she inspected and found the name Lily on her collar.

"All girls so far. I wonder, though, if that big old shepherd out there has a name tag somewhere?" Back in the kitchen, she leaned down and petted the shepherd on the head. "Let's see who you are?" No collar on the dog's neck left her feeling a little disappointed, but it was short-lived when she realized the dog was lying on a bed someone had taken the time to cross-stitch the name Jack on.

"Jack? Is that your name?" The shepherd licked her hand and placed his paw in it. "Okay, now that we've all established names, I think I should eat. My stomach is growling like it hasn't had food in a year. It was a long drive this morning."

After eating her sandwich at the table, Maddie threw the wrapper into the garbage and finished her bottle of water. Realizing she still had a few hours to burn until Kyle and his helper came home, Maddie stood up. The beach was calling her name, but first she had to figure out how to get past the geese.

At her car, she pulled out her bag and the pair of sneakers she packed along with shorts and a tee. After changing into them in the house, she placed the other clothes back into the bag in the car. No since keeping them in the house when she would be looking for a motel room later.

Rounding the corner of the house, Maddie stopped and looked around. Not a goose in sight, but that did not mean a thing. They were probably waiting for her to make an appearance and would jump out when she least expected it. *Ha! I'm on to you buggers*, she thought. *No way am I going to let you guys stop me now.*

With a quick jump, Maddie raced along the path and only seconds later heard the loud honking and flapping of wings behind her. But she was faster and in no time at all, they gave up and squawked back to the direction of where they had been hiding.

***

A smile on her face, Maddie followed the same path she had followed so many years ago. The trees had grown a lot and, where she once used to see the water in the distance, she could not. A few hundred feet later, though, she was standing on the outcrop of ledges overlooking the ocean below.

The smell of the Atlantic was far different than it was in Boston. Occasionally, she would wander down to South Boston and walk around the John F. Kennedy Presidential Library, but often, it wasn't enough. In the last twenty years, she really had not experienced the coast—at least not like this.

Following the path which would take her down to the beach, Maddie was soon slipping off her shoes and testing the water with her toes. How many times had she done that when she was younger? She and her aunt would spend hours down here. Sometimes they would bring a picnic lunch and make the day of it. It was where she learned to swim, and occasionally get to see seals, which had been her favorite animal as a kid.

Choosing a spot to sit in front of a large piece of driftwood, she surveyed the scenery. It was nothing but open ocean in front of her. When she was a little girl, she wanted to live here. She realized it really could be all hers now. But not without stipulations. Sal had told her if she accepted the inheritance, she would not be able to sell it. Daisy wanted to make sure Kyle always had a home and, whoever accepted the inheritance, had to be in it for the long haul.

Leaning back onto the driftwood, Maddie closed her eyes. The sun beat down on her face and the salty air assaulted her senses. Could it really be that simple to just accept the inheritance? She could enjoy this every day, but it came with other stipulations. She didn't know if she was ready to take on the responsibility of Kyle or anything else for that matter.

Chapter Three

What seemed like only seconds later, Maddie stirred. Something was crawling on her. With a yelp, Maddie swatted at her face and opened her eyes. Standing directly in front of her was a man holding a piece of dried seaweed. He was too close, and Maddie screeched, jumping up quick, which, in turn, caused him to fall backward onto the sand.

"What are you doing? Who are you?" Maddie whispered and stepped back, almost tripping over the log behind her. With wide eyes, she stared at him, waiting for him to answer and wondering if there was anything she could grab nearby to defend herself.

"Sorry. I'm Lincoln Davies, Kyle's social worker. Well, farmhand at the moment, but you know. I work with Kyle," he replied, and Maddie relaxed a little.

Maddie squinted her eyes. "Do you enjoy scaring people?"

Lincoln shook his head. "Not at all. It's…you were leaning back asleep and… I thought…never mind. It doesn't matter. I am sorry I startled you."

"Startled me? You scared me! I thought I had some type of monstrous bug crawling on me!" Maddie swiped at her hair again and then shook the sand off her clothing.

Lincoln took a step back and apologized again. "Only a piece of seaweed! I really am sorry. Maddie, is it?"

Maddie nodded her head, but she was still feeling a little leery of him. Now, if she had met him at a coffee house or with a friend, she would definitely be giving him a second look. His hair was blond, and he needed a haircut. He was in shape. And, well, it really did not matter. She would be leaving soon, so his looks really should not matter at all.

"Yes, I'm Maddie. I guess I fell asleep. It's been a long twenty four hours," she told him.

Lincoln held out his hand to her. "Let's start over. I'm Lincoln Davies. I help with Kyle."

"Sal said I shouldn't expect you 'til four, though. That's why I came down here. Otherwise, I would have waited at the house."

"It's fine. I got out of a meeting and figured I would come back and get some chores done. When I didn't find you in the house, I figured you would be down here. This is Kyle's favorite place. However, why don't we go back, and I can give you a quick tour."

Wiping more sand from her legs and shorts, she stated, "I met the dogs. I hope it's not a problem that I went inside."

Lincoln chuckled. "Not at all. After all, this place is yours now."

She quickly replied, "Not yet."

"Wait. You didn't sign the paperwork today? Don't tell me you are thinking about not accepting your inheritance? What about Kyle?"

Maddie shrugged her shoulders. "I don't know what I am going to do yet. Let's just go back now, okay?"

Navigating the path back up the ledge, Maddie was fully aware of Lincoln who was directly behind her and wished she had the sense to let him go first. While she remembered every step of the way, the idea of him watching her made her stumble a few times. When she came within sight of the farmhouse, Maddie stopped and turned to Lincoln. She was not one to ask for help, but she did not want to deal with the geese again.

"The geese get you?" Maddie heard the laughter in the voice behind her.

"No. I outran the little buggers. Just wondering where they are," she retorted.

"Watch this and learn," he teased, and he walked over to a maple tree and picked up a big coffee can. Reaching inside, he grabbed some pellets and held out his hand for her to see. "Distraction!" he declared and then called out, "Come on, Lucy! Ricky! We're coming!" He then started walking toward the house with Maddie close behind him.

Within seconds, the geese were coming right at them and Lincoln threw the treats to the side. They followed the treats and he and Maddie quickly scooted past them.

"I wish I'd known that before. I haven't done marathon running in a long time. I didn't realize how fast geese are!" she said.

Grinning, Lincoln grabbed her hand and pulled her around the front of the house. "Did you go to the barn?" Maddie shook her head and he continued. "There's definitely something there you are going to like better than the geese."

The barn structure was relatively new and painted the traditional barn-red color. With five stalls on each side, it could easily house several animals. Maddie noted the doors on each end as well as a ladder going up to what appeared to be a loft for storing hay.

It did not take long for her to notice what Lincoln was trying to show her in the first stall. Maddie gasped. "Babies? You have baby goats?

Lincoln's mouth turned upward. "No. You have goats, Maddie. Come meet Lady A and her twins, Elsa and Anna. The other one is Betty. She's the milking goat."

"Elsa and Anna? Seriously?"

Lincoln nodded his head. "Daisy let the neighbor's little girl name them. She is really big into the Disney movie. And Daisy loved the girls, so…"

"Why does…did…why goats? And cows?" Maddie questioned. "She only had pets and chickens when I was little."

"Did Sal tell you at all about the farm and what Daisy has been doing?" he questioned.

Maddie shook her head. "Um…he didn't really say too much…just that I wouldn't have to worry about money and…he told me a little about Kyle. I don't think he said anything about all these animals or what exactly Daisy was doing. The last time I was here, Aunt Daisy only had chickens. And dogs. She always loved dogs. But this? I don't get it."

"You miss her?" Lincoln asked softly.

Maddie snapped, "I've missed her every damned day for almost twenty years. Did you know that? My parents told me my Aunt Daisy died about twenty years ago! Then

I get a phone call telling me she just died." Maddie then burst into tears and ran out the barn door.

***

Maddie wiped the tears from her eyes as she watched Lincoln walking toward her. Something about him unsettled her. It was not like her to be nervous around someone. People did not intimidate her. She did not care who they were. Maybe it was his rough around the edges looks or his piercing blue eyes. Or maybe it was the fact that he seemed so comfortable around her. Tickling her to wake her up? Who does that with a complete stranger?

What irritated her more than ever, though, was that he saw her cry. She was not a crier. And, if she did cry, she did not do it in front of strangers. Or anybody for that matter. Not her. Everyone always told her she was a tough cookie and, if what she heard was true, she was earning herself the nickname of Ice Queen.

Lifting her head up, she figured the best way to deal with Lincoln was to be completely honest and upfront about everything.

"Sorry for breaking down." Taking a deep breath, she added, "I didn't sleep much last night."

Lincoln sat down beside her on the step. "I can understand that. Perfectly normal for the circumstances, I'm sure." Reaching out, Lincoln grabbed her hand in his.

Stifling the urge to rip her hand away, Maddie inhaled through her nose and exhaled through her mouth. Her hand felt all tingly and warm. Her face felt hot, too, and she stifled a groan. The last thing she needed was to be attracted to Lincoln. Especially Lincoln.

Standing up, she pulled her hand away from him. Him and his dirty-blond, too-long hair, his blue eyes, and his crooked smile made her nervous. She had no idea why. She worked with plenty of attractive men, but they had never given her this feeling. Maybe it was stress, and she did not get enough sleep. That had to be it.

Exasperated, she looked around her and threw her hands up in the air. "I really don't know what I am doing. I don't know anything about animals, farming, or even Kyle. I do know Sal said he had Down Syndrome, but let me tell you, I don't know much about it. I did a charity once to help raise money for Down Syndrome. That doesn't make me an expert. So, where does that leave me? Taking on the responsibility of all of this without anything or anyone to back me up." Looking at him head on, she asked, "What would you do?"

Lincoln returned her gaze and did not hesitate to answer. "Learn. Ask questions. Find out exactly what all of this involves. Get to know Kyle—on his good days and his bad days. Then make your decision—an educated decision."

"Sounds easy, but I don't have that kind of time. I have to be back in Boston by Monday."

"You cannot possibly make a decision by then. Monday?" Lincoln asked, obviously confused by the timeline or lack of time for her to decide what she was going to do.

Maddie sighed and sat back down. "Yeah, Monday. My boss told me to take the time I need, but she's…let's just say she didn't mean it. Taking today off will probably mean I'm out of the running for a promotion."

Lincoln remained silent. *Well, he's certainly a big talker*, she thought. Daring a quick glimpse over at him, she found him staring at her. "What?" she demanded.

"At this point, you have to consider your inheritance. Not only will you get all this, but you will also get to build a relationship with your cousin. Kyle is an amazing kid. Kyle does not do complex. It's either black or it's white. There is no in-between. He's kind. He's generous. He is serious a lot of the time, but he loves to have fun and make people laugh. He can change your life for the better…if you allow it to happen. That's it, though. You have to allow it to happen, and I don't see it happening on your short timeline."

Maddie's eyes rested on her feet. She worked her butt off at the agency, but ask if she loved her job and she would have to say no. It was a job. Friends were hard to come by at the agency because everyone seemed to be out for themselves. There was no camaraderie at all and, by the time five o'clock rolled around, she was ready to go home and forget about work until she returned the next morning. If she got the promotion the only changes she could foresee was the fact she would be working a lot more hours. But still, this was all she had in her life since she lost her family.

She and Phoenix had not been close, and it was something she always regretted. With over six years between them, they were both at different places in their development. But when Phoenix had died in a car accident on prom night of her senior year, it had changed Maddie's world. Her parents quickly went from the loving, kind, and observant parents to parents who did not even realize she existed. They had been heartbroken and Maddie, only twelve years old, had to learn how to deal with things by herself.

At eighteen, her father had died of a heart attack, and Maddie secretly believed it was due to his heart being broken over Phoenix. Her mother passed two, short years later after a late diagnosis of pancreatic cancer. She had given up long before the diagnosis, so Maddie had not been surprised to find herself alone at the age of twenty. It was upsetting to find out her Aunt Daisy could have been a part of her life. If only she had known.

With a catch in her throat, she whispered to Lincoln, "I don't know if I can."

Lincoln stood up and stepped down to the ground in front of her. "Well, let's not get you upset over your decision. Let's take one step at a time and see what happens. I actually have to head back into town to pick up Kyle from work in about an hour. Do you want to get settled into your room first? I can show you the way."

"My room? I figured I would find a motel for the night."

Lincoln laughed. "Absolutely not! Daisy would want you right here, and I know Kyle will feel the same way. On top of that, you won't find a motel within thirty or forty minutes from here. The only inn we have in Cove's Port is sitting empty, waiting for someone to buy it. No place to stay but here."

Hesitating, she asked, "You think so?" The last place she wanted to be was somewhere where she was not wanted.

"Well, he might not show it much, but he is looking forward to getting to know you. Kyle can have some issues with change and Daisy's death has caused him to act out a bit, but I am sure we'll take a few steps forward soon. You've just got to be patient with him. There isn't any need to rush things."

Maddie had never been accused of being patient in her life. She had always been in a hurry to get where she was going, even if she did not know her destination. Even Kyra told her to slow down and take some time to enjoy life. She just didn't know if she was capable of slowing down.

Maddie stood up and wiped the back of her shorts off. "Well, if I am staying here, you might as well show me where I'll be sleeping."

Lincoln's lips did a quick upward turn, and he clapped his hands together. "Yes! Thank you, Maddie. You're not going to regret this."

Feeling the knots forming in her stomach, she was not sure whether the cause was the prospect of meeting Kyle soon or Lincoln's smile. All she knew was she was staying the night here at the farm, and the thought terrified her.

It was not until she started to walk up the stairs behind Lincoln that the memories started to hit her. Rubbing her hand over the flowery wallpaper, she remembered the summer she and Aunt Daisy put it up.

"That's it, Maddie. Just go from the middle to the edge. That will get those air bubbles out and we'll have beautiful flowers to look at every time we come upstairs," her aunt had said to her.

"But, Aunt Daisy, it's hard. They're bubbles. Can't I just pop them?" she remembered asking.

"Well, you would think that would be easy, but then you will have a hole in the paper. Do you want holes in the paper, Maddie?"

Maddie had laughed and said, "No, Aunt Daisy. Holes would look funny!"

Lincoln's voice broke in, "You okay?"

Maddie wiped tears from her eyes and blinked a few times. "I'm fine. I was remembering when my aunt and I put up this old wallpaper."

"You used to come here a lot?"

"Every summer until I was nine. I was supposed to come that summer, but…I never got to and then..." Seeing the confusion on Lincoln's face, she added, "My parents told me she died. I didn't know—until now."

Lincoln stepped forward. "You really thought she was dead? I mean before now? I thought that's what you said outside, but I didn't want to press it."

Maddie nodded her head, not caring whether the tears were falling or not. She still could not believe she had missed out on twenty years of her aunt's life. Why would her parents tell her that? Something wasn't right, and she was determined to find out what.

"I assumed you'd had a falling out or something. I'm sorry." Lincoln's voice was low, and he moved closer to her. "This must be so hard for you."

After wiping away the tears, Maddie took a deep breath and continued. "I honestly don't know what happened. I was nine-years-old and I was supposed to come visit Aunt Daisy after my sister did. But then my sister wanted to stay for the whole summer and my parents let her. So, I didn't get to come because school had already started.

The next week, my parents told me Aunt Daisy died. They never told me how…they just said she was gone. I was devastated." She whispered the last sentence. "If only I'd known. Both of my parents died within a short time of each other. If I had known she was alive, I would have come back. I certainly wouldn't have waited until she was gone."

"You didn't know. You were a little girl when it happened. When you are young, you take the information given to you and accept it. It isn't until we get older that we begin to question things, especially what our parents tell us."

"Yeah, but I should have asked more questions about how she died and why we never went to her funeral," she snapped. She watched Lincoln's eyes narrowed and her shoulders sagged. "I'm sorry."

Lincoln touched her arm. "No harm done. I get it. You're stressed. However, when Kyle comes home, you are going to have to do your best to keep it together or you're going to freak him out. He's not used to any type of stress, so this has hit him hard. He really misses her."

Maddie nodded her head. Of course, Kyle was stressed. He had lost his mother. He was only twenty and, on top of that, he may have some cognitive disabilities. All of this must have been so devastating to him. How on earth was she supposed to handle all of this when she could not even handle her own emotions?

Chapter Four

Maddie followed Lincoln to one of the doors when he stated, "This is Kyle's room." A small bark came from inside, and he opened it. Within seconds, a small black and white dog came to the door. "Maddie, meet Mutley. This is Kyle's dog, and Mutley will not come out of the room without him."

Maddie leaned down and held her hand out for the dog to sniff. "Oh, Mutley! You are a cutie." She then asked Lincoln, "What happens if you leave the door open?"

Lincoln chuckled. "He doesn't stop barking. He prefers the door shut. It used to drive Daisy nuts. Mutley won't even come outside to do his duty unless Kyle takes him. Kyle takes his responsibility for Mutley very seriously."

Maddie stood up as the dog wandered back in the room and jumped up on Kyle's bed. He sat down in the middle and stared at them. Maddie didn't know whether to laugh or be concerned. "Loyalty is a great characteristic, but I think Mutley might be taking it too far."

"He's been that way since Kyle brought him home from the shelter. The bond between the two is unbelievable." Reaching over, he pulled the door shut. "I've got a little bit before I have to go get Kyle from work. You have two choices in rooms. I've been staying in this one across from Kyle's, but you've got Daisy's room you can stay in or the one at the very end. It's small, but clean."

He then opened the door to Daisy's room, and Maddie closed her eyes and took a deep breath. Squaring her shoulders, she stepped forward into the room.

"It hasn't changed a bit," Maddie whispered. She added, "I remember coming in here when I was little. I used to try out her makeup and brush my hair while she wrote in her journals every night."

Maddie's eyes scanned the room. "Um, no. I don't want to upset Kyle. Honestly, if someone barged in my house when my mother had died and wanted to take over her things, I would have been wild. I can't do that to him or anyone." Maddie came back out of Daisy's room and walked down the hall to the end where her room would be, stopping in front of the door. "This is the room I slept in when I was little. I always loved the view of the backyard."

Opening the door, Maddie felt the tears well up in her eyes. Not much had changed in the twenty years since she had been in the room. Yes, the bed cover had changed, but it was the same bed, the same worn nightstand and dresser, and even the same small desk in front of the window overlooking the backyard. So many memories came at her at once.

"Aunt Daisy, I want to live with you forever," young Maddie whimpered.

"Oh, Madelyn! You have to go home tomorrow. School starts in a week, and you know how your mother is. She is going to have you model all of the new clothes she bought you. And you know what? That will make you happy. It's okay to be happy here and be happy at home. Maybe we

will see if you can stay a little longer next summer? I'd love to have you here for longer."

Reaching out, Maddy pulled her Aunt Daisy closer. She always smelled of baking and what could only be described as sunshine.

"You okay?" Lincoln stepped into the room behind her.

A quick wipe of her eyes and Maddie looked him right in the eyes. "Just memories. When I was little, I always dreamed someday I would live here with Aunt Daisy. She was…she was everything to me." After a deep breath, she smiled. "I'm good. Don't worry. I promise I'll keep it under control with Kyle. And speaking of Kyle, aren't you supposed to go get him?"

Lincoln nodded. "Yes. I am leaving right now. Do you need anything while I'm out? Do you want to come with me?"

Maddie's eyes grew wide, but nothing came out of her mouth.

"It's not a problem if you don't. In fact, why don't you stay here and get settled. That will give me another chance to talk to Kyle about you and reassure him everything is going to be okay. He knows about you and why you are here, but I can reassure him you are not some green-eyed monster ready to whisk him away from his home."

"Is that what he thinks?" Maddie gulped.

Lincoln's eyes never left hers. "Honestly, I don't know what he thinks right now. But this will give me a chance to reassure him you are here to help and you are a nice person. Like I said before, Kyle will get used to the idea of you being around. But it will take some time."

"I'll stay here…get my stuff from the car. And give you a chance to talk, but don't you think Kyle would prefer me to stay at a hotel?" she asked.

"No. That would only make matters worse. Like I said, Kyle knows why you are here." Lincoln turned around to leave and then added, "Maybe after Kyle goes to bed tonight, we can find some time to sit down and talk about him. I'll fill you in on everything, so you at least have that info before you make a decision."

Another look of panic crossed Maddie's face, and Lincoln gave her a quick smile. "I'll be back shortly."

As soon as she heard the door slam downstairs, Maddie sat down on the bed. How was she going to do this? Being back here in Aunt Daisy's house had her in tears every second. She knew she needed to keep it together for Kyle while she was here, but she was not sure if she could pull it off. How was she supposed to look after Kyle when she could barely take care of herself?

Heck, she could not even keep a relationship going with anyone but her friend, Kyra. She had not dated in months and, sadly, it did not really matter. She had not met anyone she was remotely interested in. Apart from coworkers and Lincoln, she had not even talked to a man in a long time.

And now she was attracted to Lincoln. He was obviously a nice guy. But nice guys and her did not do well. The few she had dated complained incessantly about her absenteeism, and that was where the rumors of Ice Queen started. It was not that she did not want a relationship. She did. The right time and the right guy had not happened. Yet. She was still holding out hope. Just not with Lincoln. A country boy and city girl would never work out.

Feeling foolish for letting her thoughts stray, Maddie took a deep breath. Kyle would be home soon. Palms sweaty, she glanced in the small mirror hanging above the dresser. She looked as frazzled as she felt. Time to get her things and at least make herself more presentable or Kyle would quickly see exactly how stressed she was.

Chapter Five

Maddie stretched and lay in the bed with the cool breeze coming in through the window she had opened during the night. The unmistakable crow of a rooster sounded off once more, and she smiled. She had not heard that sound in years. The last summer she was at the farm, the crow was her signal to get out of bed. Aunt Daisy had always been an early riser and, more often than not, had beaten the rooster. No matter what time the rooster crowed, she would always have breakfast ready for Maddie when she clamored down the stairs.

While the memories were pleasant, she only wished her Aunt Daisy were here now. She knew Lincoln had done his best to make the meeting between her and Kyle easy and pleasant, but in her eyes, it had been a disaster. Nothing she said or did was right. Kyle had been shy and the whole thing had seemed awkward. About the time Lincoln said it was time to get the animals into the barn, she had overreacted.

"You want me to what?" she asked.

Kyle had stood in front of her. "It's okay, Maddie. We need to bring in the animals for the night."

"I…Okay, let me change," she grumbled. After going upstairs and throwing on a pair of jeans, she had come back downstairs to find the house empty. Knowing she would probably find them out in the barn, she had marched out of the house. When she came to the barn, she had pulled the barn door open only to be sideswiped by a cow.

Kyle had yelled, "Watch out!"

Lincoln yelled, "Shut the door!"

The cow had simply pushed by her, hard enough to throw her off balance and she…well, she had landed on her rear end in a pile of fresh manure. Lincoln and Kyle had just stood there in the barn laughing. They had actually laughed at her. Humiliated, she had stood up only to find herself slip and fall back down in it. Lincoln, of course, had come over to help her get up, but when he stood in front of her with laughter in his eyes, it only made her mad.

"You think this is funny? Do you know how much these jeans cost me?" She finally managed to get up on her own, not daring to try to brush any of the manure off her for fear of making it worse.

Lincoln turned to Kyle when his face suddenly became serious. He leaned in and whispered, "Careful. Kyle is watching us. Let's get you cleaned up. It's no big deal. Cow manure is basically chewed up grass and hay."

"Just chewed up grass and hay? It's probably staining my clothes right now," she squealed. She normally would not have cared, but she worked hard for her money and, while it might have been on a whim, she had spent almost a quarter of her weekly paycheck on the jeans that were now covered in crap.

When she glanced Kyle's way, all she could see was his back as he walked out of the back door of the barn into the pasture. Knowing she had blown it, she glared at Lincoln and headed back to the house. Let them round up all the animals on their own. She groaned. Let them do it all the time, because after what happened, she knew there was no way on earth she could accept her inheritance. Farm life for Maddie Jones who grew up in a city? Absolutely not. There was no way she was spending her time cleaning up crap and who knew what else.

Dinner was even more awkward after the barn incident. Lincoln had gone into town to pick up a couple of pizzas leaving Kyle and her at home. Kyle had begged to go, but Lincoln had been firm. "No. You should stay with Maddie and show her where to find everything in the kitchen."

Kyle had stomped his feet and protested, "All she has to do is look in the cupboards. I don't want to stay with her."

Maddie could not really blame him. She had basically acted like a sissy. Like a girl from the city who couldn't handle a little bit of cow manure. She had made a big deal out of nothing and now she was going to pay. Kyle didn't want anything to do with her, and she really couldn't blame anyone but herself.

She did try, though, to make amends with him. "Kyle, maybe we can sit and talk while Lincoln goes to the store. I would love to hear more about your mother and you."

Kyle had shaken his head and marched upstairs with Mutley following close at his heels.

Lincoln said, "Don't worry about it. It doesn't take much to set Kyle off right now. He misses Daisy, and he hates change. Give it some time. He will forget all about it."

"We don't have a lot of time, Lincoln. I have to be back to work on Monday," she stated.

Lincoln let out his breath. "I should be back in a few. Just leave Kyle be. He'll be down when the pizza arrives."

For the next twenty minutes, Maddie stood at the bottom of the stairs listening to the noises coming from above. She was not sure if Kyle was talking to Mutley or himself, but he was not happy. She could not make out the words, which was probably a good thing, but the one thing she was certain of was Kyle hated her. Nothing she did or said would matter to him; he had made up his mind about her and that was that.

Lincoln walked through the door to find her at the bottom of the steps and put the pizza on the table. With a smile on his face, he stepped closer to listen. Upon hearing Kyle's voice, he laughed. "Mutley's his best friend. He's got to vent to someone."

Maddie was speechless. Didn't Kyle's actions concern Lincoln at all? Was that Kyle's normal behavior? She did not know if she had the capability…or patience…to deal with it. Would that happen every day with him? Or was it only because she was here?

Looking at Lincoln, she whispered, "I don't think I can do this. I…"

Lincoln reached out and grabbed her by the shoulders. "You would be surprised by what you can do. I promise tomorrow will be better. Kyle will have forgotten about all of this. I promise."

Maddie wanted to believe it. It was not that she thought farm life was for her. It was the fact that this was her aunt's farm. Her aunt loved this place, and she loved Kyle. Maddie did not want to let her aunt down, but if Kyle hated her, what else could she do? Staying did not really seem to be an option right now.

The pizza was eaten with Lincoln trying to engage both she and Kyle into some kind of small talk. Kyle simply ate his pizza, ignoring both of them for the most part. Every now and then she would catch him sneaking a small piece of crust to Mutley who lay on the floor by Kyle's feet. Once he had eaten his fill, Kyle asked to be excused to take Mutley for a walk.

Lincoln had then taken it upon himself to fill her in about Kyle's medical conditions. "He does have a congenital heart defect, and he goes in for a yearly checkup. Right now, things look rather good, but the situation can change. Should you decide to accept your role as his guardian, I would recommend getting copies of his medical records and going over them yourself."

"What does that mean? Congenital heart defect?" she asked.

Lincoln leaned back in his chair. "I'm sure you've heard of babies being born with a hole in their heart? That's basically what it is. It is a defect, and for Kyle, it meant surgery at six days old and then again when he turned ten."

Maddie could not imagine what her aunt went through in having an infant go in for heart surgery or even a young boy. "What about now? Can it cause problems for him now?"

"I think you always have to be aware of the issue, but from what I understand Kyle's surgery was successful. However, you also have to worry about other heart diseases. He has a higher risk of cardiovascular disease. That is why we try to keep him active and watch his weight. We try to make sure he is eating healthy. Yeah, we had pizza tonight, but did you notice it was all veggies? Daisy was always careful to make sure Kyle got extra fruit and vegetables in his diet. He also has poor vision, but it's corrected with his glasses. Daisy always kept on top of his medical needs."

"I can see why. How did she do this? I mean, Aunt Daisy would have been forty when she adopted Kyle. That's not exactly young and then to take on a sick child at that. I can't imagine." Maddie realized this was a part of her aunt's life she knew nothing about. She had seen her aunt only three to four times a year and spent a short time with her in the summer. Beyond that, her aunt's life remained a mystery.

"She loved him," Lincoln told her. "Love is worth it no matter how hard it is. And you must remember Kyle is not Down Syndrome. He is a young man *with* Down Syndrome. Down Syndrome does not define who he is. He is a person with a genetic disorder. Your aunt thought he was perfect just the way he is."

Maddie nodded her head, but inside she was reminded she had never really felt this way about anything or anyone before. Yes, she had loved her sister and her parents. Unfortunately, she had never really felt a connection with any of them, and after her sister Phoenix had died, her relationship with her parents had only gotten worse.

For the next hour, Lincoln reviewed Kyle's history with her, upcoming appointments, and things Lincoln was working on for Kyle. "While the goal is always independence, for Kyle complete independence is not possible. Being quite honest with you, Kyle's current development is at an approximate age of ten. You wouldn't leave a ten-year old to make decisions about life on their own. Kyle simply needs someone to guide him through and help him to make the best decisions possible. Daisy taught him to do a lot most ten-year-olds would never do, so in this sense, he is further ahead than where he would be without her guidance."

How could she, Maddie Jones, guide someone else and help them when her own life was in shambles? Maybe not shambles—she knew she was exaggerating in her own mind, but still, her life was far from perfect. She worked at a job she tolerated. She lived in a tiny apartment. She had no social life whatsoever, because all her time was put into trying to further her career. How was she, of all people, supposed to guide someone else to make the right life choices when she could not even make the right choices for herself?

Maddie hung her head while Lincoln watched her from across the table. When Kyle walked in from his walk, he did not even glance her way. Lincoln was the first to say something.

"Kyle, just about time for a shower and bed. You worked hard today."

Kyle let out a grunt. "I just took one…"

"Yesterday, Kyle. You need one tonight after helping in the barn."

"Take a shower, Kyle. You stink, Kyle," was the muttered response as Kyle stomped upstairs.

Maggie had felt her mouth drop but did not realize Lincoln was staring at her until he spoke. "Don't be alarmed by Kyle talking to himself. We all do it. It is just more pronounced with him. Sometimes he does it to remind himself of something he has to do. Other times, like now, he is doing it to help him handle the situation. When he is mad about something, it calms him down."

Maddie understood it but having never been this involved with anyone with Down Syndrome, it was a new experience for her. Now, lying in bed, she was determined to make today matter. One way or another, she had to come to her decision about what she was going to do about her inheritance. Even if Kyle were not involved, she did not think she could sell the farm. It held too many good memories for her to just toss aside. But it was more than the farm. It was Kyle. He needed someone he could count on. Yet, she did not think she was that someone. Heck, she freaked out when she got cow manure on her. How was she supposed to handle a major crisis?

Chapter Six

Not sure what the morning chores would be, Maddie took her time getting ready. She was not afraid of hard work, but she didn't want a repeat of last night. She was determined to make the best of today and see if there was any progression with Kyle. A quick glance in the mirror revealed she at least looked half-way decent. No use for her *Jimmy Choo's* this morning. She dressed in a pair of jeans, sneakers, and an over-sized sweatshirt. Thankfully, she had come prepared for anything.

As she crept down the stairs, she found Lincoln waiting at the bottom. She whispered, "Is Kyle up yet? I tried to be quiet. I didn't want to wake him."

"No, but he should be soon. The latest that boy ever sleeps is seven. If he's not up by then, I'll go wake him up myself. Coffee?" he asked.

"Definitely. I forgot what it was like to sleep here. I don't think I've slept that good for years. It must be the fresh air," Maddie said and then waited for him to pass her a cup.

"Cream? Sugar?" he asked.

Taking a sip, she then shook her head. "Just musses up the flavor of the coffee." With a quick and self-conscious laugh, she added, "Musses? I haven't heard that word in ages. I can't believe I used it. It must be the country atmosphere."

Lincoln laughed. She noticed how it was not only his mouth that appeared to laugh. His eyes, a bright blue, lit up.

"What would you like to do today? Kyle and I will do the morning chores right after breakfast and then we're wide open. Do you want to do anything special?"

Maddie glanced around the kitchen and back to Lincoln. "I'd honestly like to just take some time to look around today. I know my aunt was a list maker. I thought if I looked through some of her stuff it would help me make a decision. If you and Kyle don't mind, that is?"

Lincoln nodded his head. "I don't see why it would be a problem. Why don't you start right after breakfast while we do the chores and then maybe later on, we'll have time to do something? Like go get Kyle an ice cream or take him down to the beach?"

Maddie took another sip of coffee and returned his smile. "Sounds good."

The sound of the door opening upstairs alerted them both to Kyle's impending arrival, and Lincoln turned back to the stove. "Breakfast?" he asked.

"Coffee is enough for right now. Thanks," Maddie replied quietly as Kyle came down the stairs.

"Good morning, Lincoln. Good morning, Maddie. Mutley has to go pee. I'll be right back." Kyle, dressed in a pair of denim shorts and a red t-shirt, wore the biggest smile on his face as he opened the door.

Maddie's face changed from one of trepidation to awe. "Seriously? I was scared to come downstairs this morning afraid that Kyle wouldn't speak to me after yesterday."

"The wonderful thing about Kyle is that he is very forgiving. Give him a few hours. That's all it takes. Too bad we all couldn't work that way."

Maddie stood up and walked to the counter. "Mind if I grab another cup? I need at least two to get me going in the morning." After filling her cup, she whispered to Lincoln, "Should I ask if he minds if I go in Daisy's room?"

"Why don't you just go in when we head out to the barn? Or let me bring it up to him? I'll keep Kyle busy for at least an hour or two. It will give me a chance to get the pig pen a little sturdier. I know Sam got out one day and I swear the whole town showed up to help Daisy catch him."

Maddie's eyebrows rose. "Sam?"

"The boar. He's going to market in the fall. I remember Daisy talking about it a few weeks ago. There is also a litter out there. I think two are spoken for already, but there are six more that will need to be sold." Lincoln looked out the window, his back to her. "I came over to see her about Kyle's work schedule, and she was talking to the processor. That was the last time I saw her."

Maddie heard the break in Lincoln's voice. "I'm sorry I didn't realize how close you were."

"The funny thing is that your aunt was more than her eccentricities. Daisy loved to talk and, to be honest, a lot of people avoided her because of it. Even if you saw her the day before, she could talk for hours before remembering she had things to do. She had a big heart, though, and was always helping people out."

Walking up beside him, Maddie looked out the window. The trees had grown a lot over the years and, what was once a small water view, was now a view of birch trees.

While most people would have probably cut them down to retain the view, not Aunt Daisy. She wouldn't harm a tree to clear the view.

"You know, I didn't know Aunt Daisy as an adult. It's nice to hear stories from people who did. I'm sure she considered you a friend." She reached out and touched his arm. "I know Kyle does, too." Glancing at the clock, she asked, "Time for another cup?"

After pouring another cup for Lincoln, Maddie watched Kyle walk through the door and grab a plate from the cupboard. Filling the plate with the food Lincoln had prepared, Kyle then sat down at the table with Mutley curled up by his feet.

"After you eat breakfast, I think we need to clean out the barn and the hen house is probably due for it, too," Lincoln said.

Kyle did not say a word—just grunted, picked up his toast, and started eating.

"Maybe if we can get them done this morning, we can go down to the beach later. What do you think?"

Kyle chewed fast and, before he could swallow, muttered, "Is Maddie going to help?"

Maddie's eyes grew wide. Lincoln chuckled. "No. Let's give Maddie time to get used to the farm before we have her cleaning up after the animals. I think it would be good if she went in your mother's room and started to clean up in there a little bit. What do you think?"

Kyle's fork stopped midair. After a quick glance at Maddie, he nodded his head and whispered, "Can I have Mummy's quilt?"

Maddie's lips turned down and she reached out to touch Kyle's hand. "Of course, you can. You can have anything you want out of her room. I promise not to throw anything out before checking with you."

Kyle flinched at the contact and Lincoln held his breath. "Maddie won't throw anything away without asking. Maddie won't throw anything away without asking."

Before Kyle could repeat the statement again, Lincoln spoke up. "It's okay, Kyle. She won't. Once we are done with the barn, we will get the quilt and anything else you want to keep." Kyle instantly relaxed and continued eating until his plate was empty.

Maddie watched Kyle eat and slowly let out a breath. She could not fall apart in front of him and carefully wiped a tear from her eye. Right now, she saw nothing but raw pain in that boy's eyes. Pain she did not want to add to, and she vowed to keep her own emotions under control.

As soon as Kyle got up from the table, he rinsed the dish off in the sink and put it in the dishwasher. After going to the cupboard and pulling out an assortment of dog food bags, he then pulled a set of dishes out of the cupboard and placed them on the counter. Maddie and Lincoln exchanged glances, and Maddie felt her face getting warm when Lincoln winked.

Kyle measured a different amount of food from different bags into each of the dishes and then opened a can of dog food and divided it between the five bowls. Once it was done, he grabbed a spoon and spent a few minutes mixing them up. Without a word, he carefully placed each dish on the floor and called out the name of the dog it belonged to. In minutes, four dogs were happily eating. Peaches, however, was not at her dish and Kyle groaned.

"She's not eating again, Lincoln. Should I go get her?" Kyle asked in a whisper.

"Don't worry, Kyle. Peaches will come eat when she's hungry. Just put it back up on the counter," Lincoln replied. "She just needs some time."

Maddie could see the problem. Peaches had been Daisy's dog and seemed to be in mourning for her. If she didn't eat soon, she knew a trip to the vet might be necessary for the poor dog.

Chapter Seven

Maddie's hand trembled as she ran it over the quilt on her aunt's bed. When Kyle had said he wanted his mother's quilt, she had instantly known exactly what he was talking about. Twenty years and the memories were still as clear as if they had happened yesterday.

Lightning flashed and the bedroom lit up startling little Maddie awake. The thunder that rumbled just two seconds later had her scrambling to her feet and out the door. Her aunt's door was open, and she peeked in to find her aunt sitting up in bed reading.

"You scared, honey?" Maddie could only nod her head in response.

Aunt Daisy smiled and patted the bed beside her. Maddie crawled up on the bed and her aunt covered her over with the quilt. Then she had given her a hug and told her a story.

"Thunder and lightning are nothing to be afraid of. Do you believe in God?" she asked. Again, Maddie nodded her head.

"Well, when people die, they go to heaven. And heaven is a great place to be. You can do anything you want. Now, a lot of people like to go bowling." Looking at Maddie, she asked, "Have you ever been bowling?"

Maddie nodded and ducked further under the quilt as another loud rumble sounded off and lightning flashed in the sky.

"Well, a lot of people in heaven like to bowl. That thunder you hear is just the sound of the balls up in heaven flying down the lane to knock down the pins."

Maddie's eyes grew larger. "Then what's the lightning?"

Aunt Daisy had laughed. "The lightning, my dear, is the light that flashes when someone gets a strike. Obviously, someone up there is doing really good tonight."

In that moment in time, she had never felt as safe. As her hands ran over the quilt, she knew this quilt had probably seen Kyle through many tough nights. Standing up, Maddie approached her aunt's desk. A desk calendar covered the top and she viewed the dates and all her aunt's appointments. Today's date was empty, but on Monday there was a note with the time of ten o'clock and the initials MKT. Unsure of what that meant, she grabbed a piece of paper and wrote it down to ask Lincoln. In the month of June, there were two more appointments, but it looked like they were doctor's appointments for Kyle. July had more appointments scheduled, and Maddie figured it would be easier to bring the whole calendar downstairs with her.

A leather-bound notebook sat in the corner of the desk. Picking it up, Maddie could not help but smile. A journal. She remembered her aunt telling her journaling was her favorite thing to do. Opening it, she read the last entry.

June 19

The sun shone brightly today and as I drove Kyle into work this morning, a moose was standing in the middle of the road. Kyle's eyes lit up brighter than the sun. Definitely a great way to start the day. Kyle's love for animals grows more and more every day and I thank God every day for bringing this boy into my life. There may be days that dealing with it all is difficult, but it is the days like today that make it worth every second. Here's to tomorrow and whatever it may bring!

Skipping back a few pages, Maddie continued to read.

June 7

Thankful that God gave me the ability to make something out of nothing. The boys from the market will be here in a few weeks and I still can't believe my dream is coming true. For years, I've worked on these recipes and now look what is happening. Well, it is not happening yet, but I can guarantee that the next time I see the boys, they are going to have a contract in hand. The only problem I foresee is what I am going to do with the money. Kyle and I have everything we need. Maybe it is time to start giving some of it back? I am sure the animal shelter can use some more. Just grateful that I can do this.

Boys from the market? Contract? She was going to have to talk to Lincoln and see what he knew about this. Setting the journal down on top of the calendar to read later, Maddie surveyed the room. Her aunt was not a hoarder, by any means, but she had a lot of stuff in her room to go through. Knick-knacks and trinkets sat on top of the bureau, on shelves, and anywhere they would fit. Sure that Kyle would want to keep some of them, Maddie left them all in place.

There was no way she was heading back to Boston today. When she had first arrived, she fully expected to be on her way home within twenty-four hours. That was before she met Kyle. That was before she realized what the inheritance involved. She could not run off without speaking to Sal again, either. Grabbing her phone, she dialed the office and left a message on Wendy's voice mail. She was taking the full week off to deal with her aunt's death. And besides, there was no way she was missing her aunt's funeral on Tuesday.

Feeling a little relieved after the phone call, Maddie sorted through her aunt's clothing. She was not sure if anyone had picked out an outfit for the funeral, so she took the time to pick out a nice dress and shoes to match. Around the farm, her aunt mostly wore overalls—or at least she used to—and they were not appropriate for burial attire. After making several piles for donating, throwing, and keeping, Maddie checked the time. Still a few minutes left before she was expecting Lincoln and Kyle, so she decided to hop in the shower.

In her room, Maddie grabbed her things and glanced out the window. She did not see either Kyle or Lincoln at the barn, but who knows? Maybe they were out with the pigs. She still could not believe her aunt was raising pigs. She ate pork, and bacon was high on her list of must-haves, but to slaughter a pig to eat? Nope. This part of farm life was a turn-off for her. Eggs? No problem. She used to help her aunt collect the eggs when she stayed with her. But even cleaning out the barn seemed like a chore she was not sure she could handle. How the heck could she, Madeline Presley Jones, become a farmer?

Stepping out of her room, Maddie walked the few steps to the bathroom and opened the door. With a yelp, she quickly slammed it shut again. Lincoln! Oh my God! Wearing nothing but a towel, he looked at her and smiled. Smiled at her while her cheeks burned with embarrassment—smiled as she slammed the door as fast as she could.

"Great job, Maddie!" she muttered to herself back in her room. Of all the stupid things to do, it would have to be her who opened a bathroom door without knocking. Yeah, she could blame it on living alone and not being used to having to share a bathroom, but really, it was just stupidity. Now, if she could only find a way to get the sight of Lincoln in his towel out of her mind. Tall, broad-shouldered, and built like a Mac truck, it was not going to be easy, and Maddie had to stifle the giggle that almost escaped. Embarrassed she might have been, but blind she was not.

Twenty minutes later, she cracked the door open to her room and listened in the hallway. Tiptoeing out of her room, she listened carefully at the bathroom door. No sounds from within, but she knocked anyway. When nobody responded, she carefully opened the door and stepped in, noting there was no lock on the door. That was something she was going to have to change.

Realizing she was already making a list of things to get done around the place, Maddie's shoulders dropped. It wasn't as if she was going to be there long enough. While her name might have been first on the list for the inheritance, her aunt had clearly not been thinking right at the time. Kyle needed someone who could handle both him and the farm. She was not sure whether she was capable of handling even one of these things.

Taking the quickest and, probably, noisiest shower in her life—she was scared someone would open the door on her—all Maddie could think about was facing Lincoln. Granted, he was not exactly her usual type. Her usual type was the clean-cut, business-suit wearing man. Her usual type would not be comfortable cleaning out a barn. Heck, her usual type would not even know how to clean out a barn. But there was something about Lincoln that was appealing. Maybe it was the way his eyes lit up when he talked about Kyle? Or the way he showed empathy for what she was going through? Or maybe it was the way he looked wearing nothing but a towel hanging low on his hips? Her cheeks heated at the memory.

She knew it was not Lincoln. It was simply that she had not had a date in eons. The last one had been a blind date set up by none other than Kyra. She did not speak to her for a week afterward. Her date had it all in the looks department, but other than that, he was rude, obnoxious, and condescending. When he had found out she was working an entry-level position at her firm, he had basically lectured her on how to get a higher position. Unbuttoning her top buttons and short skirts were his first recommendation. She never gave him a chance to say anymore—just grabbed her purse and walked out of the restaurant. She only wished she had turned around to see the look on his face when she left.

Lincoln was nothing like that. Granted, she only met him the day before, but nobody could convince her Lincoln would ever act like that. His eyes revealed a quiet, empathetic soul. That thought caused her to snicker and only because she had sounded exactly like Kyra. A quiet, empathetic soul? That was something that Kyra would say.

Of course, none of that mattered because it really did not seem feasible for her to accept her inheritance. Even if it meant she would never see the farm, Kyle, or Lincoln again. She was not cut out for this life and that was that. In the next week, her only plan was to find out more about why her family told her that her Aunt Daisy was dead. That was it. No more.

***

Maddie stood at the top of the steps knowing she would have to face Lincoln at the bottom. She could hear him and Kyle below talking about going to the beach. As much as she would rather stay upstairs and not have to face Lincoln, she knew she needed time with Kyle. Even if she did not accept the inheritance, she was still Kyle's cousin and that was something she would never deny.

Before her foot hit the bottom step, Kyle was right there waiting. "Maddie, we're going to the beach. Are you coming? Do you swim? Do you have a suit?"

Maddie laughed and replied, "Slow down. Yes, to all three questions. I have my suit on under my clothes, so I am ready when you guys are."

Kyle's eyes lit up, and he jumped up and down. "I love the beach. I am a great swimmer."

"I am sure you are. When I used to come here when I was a little girl, we always spent time at the beach. I bet you spent a lot of time there growing up."

Kyle nodded his head. "Mum and me went to the beach every day. Except when it was cold and snowing."

Maddie watched as Kyle's eyes dimmed. "It's okay, Kyle. The first thing I learned after my parent's died was that it was okay to have fun. Your mother would want that. Would she want Kyle to be crying all the time?"

Kyle shook his head.

"Would she want Kyle to go to the beach and have fun swimming?"

Kyle's eyes were a little brighter as he nodded his head.

"Then let's go have some fun, Kyle," Maddie giggled.

"I have to get Mutley ready to go, too." Kyle marched off and Maddie glanced at Lincoln. She wasn't sure if she handled the situation right or not, but part of her thought it was a good sign he had brought up his mother to her.

Lincoln cleared his throat. "You did good. You let him know it was okay to talk about her and to have fun. That's exactly what he needed to hear."

Maddie's shoulders relaxed a little. Hearing it come from Lincoln meant a lot. It was not that he was being critical all the time, but she felt a little intimidated by him. He had been working with Kyle daily for a long time. He probably knew Kyle better than anyone else. And after the catastrophe in the barn last night, it felt good to do something right for a change.

Minutes later, they stepped off the porch and around the house to take the path down to the beach. Kyle led the way. Maddie held back a little, hating the thought of getting into another confrontation with the geese. It was not until she heard the honking that she came to a full stop.

Kyle did not stop. He kept walking and she watched as the two geese came charging at him, wings a flapping, and their honking getting louder. Her mouth dropped open when Kyle dropped to his knees. The two geese stopped in front of him, heads bent down to accept the gentle touch from Kyle. Kyle whispered to them and their honking quieted.

Her eyes wanted to roam to where Lincoln stood behind her, but she did not dare to miss a moment of the encounter between the young man and these two geese. To her disappointment, it was over within a few seconds as the geese quieted down and turned back to where they had come from. Kyle stood up, turned to her and Lincoln and exclaimed, "Come on! You guys are too slow!"

With a laugh, Maddie and Lincoln followed closely behind. Maddie took a risk and whispered, "Did you see that?"

Lincoln nodded his head. "I did. I didn't know about that."

"I can't believe those evil little things are so calm." She laughed.

"Come on. If you guys stop talking, we'll get there quicker," Kyle chimed in.

Maddie shrugged her shoulders and smiled at Lincoln. "Guess he's right. Let's go."

Ten minutes later, Maddie spread her blanket out on the sand while Kyle jumped in the water without any hesitation. Lincoln stood a few feet away, not quite in the water, but close enough in case Kyle should need him. Maddie could only smile. She could get used to this. She frowned at the thought. No. If she accepted the inheritance, life would not be like this all the time. She would still have to run the farm. And that was one of the biggest factors in her decision.

She had always been an animal lover, but to raise pigs for meat? Cows for milk? She did not know the first thing about it. Granted, she had never been one to back down from a challenge, but this challenge was different. If she failed, she would be failing Kyle, too. She did not want to do that.

"You going to sit there with a serious look on your face all day or are you going to have some fun?" Lincoln called out from the water.

Maddie watched as Kyle threw a ball to Lincoln, only instead of catching it, the ball smacked Lincoln right in the forehead, knocking him backwards and under the water.

Kyle screamed with delight and his laughs got louder when Lincoln jumped up from the water to go after the ball.

"Don't you get me, Lincoln!" Kyle yelled as he tried to run through the water.

"Oh, don't you worry. I'm going to get even," Lincoln retorted with a laugh. "Maybe not right now, but I will get you."

Kyle scrambled to the shore to where Maddie waited. "You better watch out, Maddie. Lincoln might get you, too."

Maddie giggled. Kyle flexed his arms to show his muscles and then stood in front of her, blocking her view of Lincoln. "Don't worry, Maddie. I will protect you!"

But, when Lincoln started for shore, Kyle let out a squeal and hid behind Maddie, which only made her laugh even harder.

"Okay, boys! Who is hungry? I am starving. Let's say we eat now and take a break?"

Lincoln nodded his head. "Sounds good to me. I am hungry."

Kyle wiped his forehead with the back of his hand. "Me, too!"

Maddie sat back on the blanket, simply enjoying the sunshine and the company. Lincoln was slowly pulling Kyle out of his shyness around her. Kyle really knew a lot about the farm and how it operated, and he loved to talk about it. Remembering back to one of her aunt's journal entries, she asked, "Kyle, do you know anything about Aunt Daisy dealing with one of the local markets about the farm?"

Lincoln opened his mouth and closed it quickly when Kyle spoke up. "Mum was going to sell her dandelion jelly and tea to the market. They wanted a bunch of stuff from her, but she told them she'd start with those."

"Really? That's amazing. Do you know which stores they were going to be in?"

Kyle shook his head. "Nah. I didn't care which stores. Mum was really excited about it. She said to me, 'Kyle, after all these years, maybe people will stop saying I'm crazy.' I laughed because Mum was crazy. She was fun!"

Maddy smiled. "She certainly was fun. I'll have to look into this and see where she was with it. We certainly want to hold up her end of the contract if there was one."

She noticed Lincoln's approving smile. "Good idea, Maddie. Kyle, do you know if your mother had any other plans coming up besides taking the pigs to slaughter in the fall?"

Kyle shook his head. "Mum put everything in her calendar. If it's not in the calendar, it's not happening. That's what she used to say."

Maddie's eyes glistened and she said, "Kyle, I want to let you know I am going to be here all week. I called my boss and let her know I would not be back until next week. I hope that's okay with you."

Kyle clapped his hands. "I'm glad you're staying, Maddie."

Maddie smiled and hoped she was doing the right thing.

Chapter Eight

Maddie examined the room and pursed her lips. It was not perfect, but she had gotten a lot done in her aunt's room. Anything deemed as garbage, she had thrown in a box in the hallway. There was not much in the box, but she could guarantee Kyle would not have a problem throwing it all away. In another box, she placed the quilt he wanted, along with several other items she thought he would enjoy keeping. She also found a small box of old letters, ticket stubs, and a few worn pictures. Maddie was sure there was probably more in it, but she hesitated, unsure of how her aunt would feel about someone touching her most personal items. Boxes were stacked in the closet, but Maddie chose to leave them there for now.

After taking the box with the quilt across the hall to Kyle's room, Maddie sat down on Daisy's bed. The room looked less cluttered, but it was still Aunt Daisy's room. Even if she decided to stay and take on the care of Kyle, she did not think it was possible to stay in this room. With a total of four bedrooms upstairs, it wasn't like she would need it anyway.

Downstairs, Maddie opened cupboard doors to get the layout of things and moved onto closets. While her aunt's house looked organized, what she found in the closets told her otherwise. It seemed her aunt never threw anything away, including empty paper towel and toilet paper rolls, cardboard, and empty jars. Whatever closet she opened did not matter—there was something in there that should have been thrown out.

If she did decide to live here, she would get everything cleaned out. She was, and always had been, the neat freak in her circle of friends. She loved Kyra with all her heart but hated to go to Kyra's as it was always cluttered and in disarray. Kyra would laugh it off and tell her if it bothered her that bad, she could clean it. She, of course, did clean it on several occasions, but soon discovered it was easier to just not go to Kyra's apartment often.

In the dining room, Maddie found Lincoln sitting at the table looking at his phone. "Everything okay?" she asked.

"Yeah, it's all good. I'm going over some dates for upcoming meetings. I've been putting some off. Now you're here, I'm going to try to squeeze some in."

"I'm so sorry. This whole thing has messed up your job, hasn't it? I hope you have a more understanding boss than I do," Maddie replied. She still didn't know where she stood with Wendy. When she went back—if she went back—she knew her promotion would be off the table.

"The boss is great. Her concern is Kyle. Same as me. Can I ask if you have made a decision yet?" he asked. He stood up and walked over to the refrigerator. Grabbing a water, he added, "I'm not pushing. Just wondering what you're thinking is all."

"What am I going to do, Lincoln? I don't know the first thing about farming, and I don't know if I want to. But I don't want to lose Kyle. If I turn down the inheritance,

Kyle is going to hold it against me. Maybe not today, but eventually, he will. But what if I accept and then I run this place into the ground? Then he'll hold that against me. I can't win, Lincoln. Nothing I do is going to work."

Lincoln walked toward her and grabbed her by the shoulders. "Look at me, Maddie. Look at my eyes. No matter what you decide, Kyle isn't going to think any less of you. He's not built that way. He's not like you and me. We judge people based on their actions. Kyle has the unique ability to not judge people and to forgive much more easily than you and I do. It's his gift."

Maddie lifted her eyes up to meet his. "You think so? I don't want him to hate me. I may not have built the most solid relationship with Kyle, but Kyle is really all I have left. After my sister died, my parents basically gave up, too."

"I'm sorry. All of this must be so overwhelming for you. You know what you need?"

"A big bottle of wine?" Maddie suggested.

"Um, no. You need a break. You are here for the week, right? Let's take a break from everything today. I don't have to get Kyle until four. That gives us exactly seven hours to play hooky. What do you say?"

Maddie could see the teasing in Lincoln's eyes, and she really wanted to not think about what she was going to do. She only had a week to figure things out, though, and even taking one day off could set her far behind. Instead of saying yes like she wanted to, she whispered, "I can't. I have to figure out what I'm going to do, and I still don't even know much about this place and my aunt's business."

Lincoln smiled. "I knew it was a long shot. What can I do to help you?"

"Honestly, just tell me what you know about this farm. That sounds like a good place to start."

"Sounds good to me. Why don't we go out in the barn and I can give you a much better tour than what you got the other night? And I promise you that you won't get dirty," he teased.

Maddie couldn't help but laugh. No, she did not want a repeat of the other night, but she did want to find out what exactly was on the farm, including the animals and what they produced. She had a feeling she only knew about half of what really happened on the farm and how it all worked.

Following Lincoln to the barn, she listened closely.

"Here we have the milking cow, and then there are a couple of beef cows that will be slaughtered for the freezer. Also, in the barn, over here in the back corner are the goats. Daisy uses the goat's milk for a lot of different things, although I am not certain of what."

"Goat's milk? That can be used for a number of things," Maddie said. The only reason she knew that was because one of her client's at work had started a new line of skin products and some of them contained goat's milk.

"The pigs are out back a little further. Right now, there are four of them and the piglets. I believe the two are going to slaughter, including Sam, will be ready to slaughter in the fall, but again, I could be wrong on this. See? I don't know exactly what is going on either. I am just…uh…going with the flow, as they say." Lincoln smiled at her and grabbed her arm to steer her around the corner.

Pigs? Two days ago, Maddie would never have guessed she would be taking a tour of a pig sty. Or a barn filled with goats. Or being chased by geese. None of that seemed possible and, yet it was not as bad as what she thought it would be. The goats were playful, and ridiculously cute and cuddly, the cows friendly, and, heck, while the geese were not friendly, she could at least say they were comical.

Still, being in charge of all this seemed a little overwhelming. What did she know about cows and goats and geese? What did she know about helping Kyle? He probably couldn't even stand her and was only tolerating her because Lincoln told him to. With a sigh, she tuned back into what Lincoln was telling her about the pigs and how big they would get.

"From what I understand, Daisy was raising the pigs as another income source, but Kyle was the one who gave her the idea. This is something you need to understand. Kyle loves this farm and everything Daisy was doing. It's his life. Yes, he works at the market, but only because it provides him the socialization he needs. He loves people. However, if Kyle had his way, he would stay home and work on the farm all day long. Daisy made her wishes very clear to me when I started up. She wants Kyle involved in the community. She always knew that someday she'd be gone, and she wanted him to feel at home in town, even if she was not around."

Maddie smiled. Daisy was always looking out for the ones she loved. Well, she used to. What upset her was the idea that Daisy was okay not to contact her for the last twenty years. What about after her parents died? Why hadn't she contacted her then? What kept her away? The Daisy she remembered never would have done that.

Maddie's heart raced. Stumbling over a rock, Maddie twisted her ankle and yelped.

"You okay?" Lincoln ran over to her and helped her up.

Maddie tested her ankle. It was fine, but she told him, "I'll be right back. I'm going to go put an icepack on it for a minute." She hoped the few minutes would help her to get her emotions under control.

***

She had spent fifteen minutes inside trying to get herself under control. Splashing cold water on her face had helped, but lingering thoughts of why her aunt did not contact her after she lost her parents plagued her. But she could not hide out forever and walked back outside to find him.

Maddie saw Lincoln before he noticed her. She found him standing in the middle of the corral while two miniature donkeys ran around him. When one got too close, he reached out to slap it on its butt, sending it scurrying away with a whinny, only for it to return for more. Lincoln's laughter was contagious, and she let a giggle escape, revealing her presence.

"You've got to be kidding! They play tag?" Maddie would not have believed it unless she had seen it with her own eyes.

"They love it!" Lincoln responded in between laughs. "I think this is Kyle's doing. How's your ankle?" One of the donkeys came running up to the fence where

70

Maddie stood. Standing directly in front of her, it tipped its head back, opened its mouth, and brayed loudly.

Startled, Maddie stepped back and laughed. To Lincoln, she said, "It's fine." Leaning toward the donkey, she asked, "What? What do you want? You're awfully cute, but do you bite?"

With an answering bray, the donkey charged back off toward Lincoln.

Donkeys? Maddie could only shake her head. Although, she would have loved all of this when she was a kid. What had happened to her? When she was a kid, she loved coming here and taking care of the chickens and the dogs. What had changed? Why had she changed?

"Wake up, Maddie! I think Marvin wants you to pet him," Lincoln called, bringing her back to reality.

The little donkey was back in front of her and rubbing his nose on the fence. Maddie could not help but laugh when she reached out her hand and the donkey rubbed against it. He was obviously used to getting attention and demanding it when none was given.

"So, this is Marvin. What's the other one's name?" she asked.

Lincoln grinned. "I don't know if I should tell you."

Maddie's right eyebrow lifted. "Why not?"

Lincoln's smile broadened. Then his face became serious. "It's Madelyn."

Maddie's mouth hung open. "She named a donkey after me?" *Well, at least she didn't forget about me*, she thought to herself. *I guess that's something*. With a shrug of her shoulders, she said, "Well, at least she is cute."

Madelyn was not having anything to do with her, though. She was completely enamored with Lincoln, who was scratching her back.

"What do you think of them?" he asked.

"I don't mean to sound like an imbecile or anything, but why donkeys? I know the pigs, goats, cows, and all the other animals have a purpose, but what is the purpose of the donkeys? It's not like she could collect eggs or milk from them."

Lincoln continued to scratch Madelyn's back while watching her face. "I honestly think it was for pure enjoyment or they could have just needed a home. I know several people in town often called Daisy up when they had a stray animal. I remember one time someone found some baby skunks after their mother was hit by a car. Daisy raised them up and let them go right behind the house."

"I remember when I was here one summer, and she had baby kittens the mother wouldn't take care of. We spent many nights feeding them every two hours. One of the best summers I had here." Maddie had not wanted to leave the kittens when it was time for her to go home, but Aunt Daisy had promised her she would send her pictures. Every week, Maddie would get mail with an update and pictures until her aunt had found them homes.

Lincoln gave the donkey a quick pat on the rump, and then walked over to open the gate. Walking over to Maddie, he said, "Come with me."

Following close behind Lincoln, Maddie was surprised when he led her to the front entryway. At one time, it had been the porch, but over time, it had been closed in and a new porch had been built onto the front. While she had noticed the place was a little cluttered, she had not really looked around too much. Two freezers lined the back wall, and there were old cupboards. Lincoln walked over to the largest of them all and opened the doors.

Inside were glass canning jars holding an assortment of things. Stepping closer, she read some of the labels. Dehydrated dandelions, dehydrated violets, and an assortment of other flowers and herbs. There were also soap making supplies and all sorts of little gadgets she knew nothing about.

"Daisy was big on saving everything and making something out of nothing. I think these were mostly what she used for soaps, but if you look in the freezers, you will find them filled with fresh cow's milk and goat's milk. You asked Kyle about a contract the other day. From what I understand, Daisy had quite the following on all this stuff, but especially her dandelion jelly and tea. If you look in the cupboards in the house and in the back room, you will probably find an assortment of both. I know you wanted to look into the contract, so you should probably go look in her office."

"Office? I must have missed that somehow." Maddie thought she had toured the whole house.

"It's a new room Daisy added. The room was built off the living room a few years ago. Easy to miss," he replied.

"Great. Maybe I can find this contract she was talking about." While contracts could change with the death of someone, she would do her best to uphold whatever it was Daisy had promised.

After following Lincoln to the office, he stepped back and allowed her to open the door. The minute she looked inside, she groaned. While the house was somewhat neat and orderly, her office was anything but. A desk sat on the far side of the ten-by-ten room and stacks of paperwork were strewn all over it.

Maggie groaned louder. "You've got to be kidding me! Where do I begin?"

Lincoln leaned in closer to her. "You've got this. Don't worry about getting things done too quickly. You've been here a day. Right now, it all seems overwhelming, but a few minutes or work per day, and this place will be organized in no time."

Maggie nodded her head. At work, her desk was always cleared before she left for the day. Nothing was out of place. The same thing at home. She knew she was a little OCD about such things, but how did her aunt work in such a mess?

"Thanks. This is a little overwhelming. I'm not sure exactly what I'm looking for, besides the contract, but I can handle this. However, before I do anything, I need to eat. You hungry?"

Lincoln glanced at the watch on his wrist. "I am. Still awhile to go before I have to pick up Kyle. You up for a jaunt into town for lunch and then we can pick up Kyle together?"

As her stomach grumbled, Maddie laughed. "I guess so. Do you mind if I change first? I smell like animals."

Lincoln lifted his arm and sniffed. "Yeah, I probably need to change, too. Meet you in ten?"

"Perfect," Maddie replied and dashed off to her room.

Upstairs, she grabbed a clean pair of jeans and t-shirt from her suitcase. No sense in dressing up. There really weren't many places in town to eat, but she was thankful she had at least packed a few extra changes of clothes. Maddie put on her sneakers and, after a quick glance in the mirror to check her hair, she grabbed her purse off the end of the bed and went downstairs to meet Lincoln.

***

Before they pulled onto Main Street, Lincoln took his eyes off the road to glance her way. "What do you feel like eating? Delia offers the best stuff and, if she doesn't have it on the menu, the chances are good she will make it for you if she can."

"Delia's? That's the coffee shop, right?"

"It is. She can make anything from sandwiches to pizza. What sounds good to you?"

Maddie smiled. "I'm starving, so anything sounds good. When I used to come here as a little girl, Carol always made me pancakes with a smiley face."

"Carol loved kids, which is why she is happy in sunny Florida now. Her daughters are there, and she is now surrounded by her six grandchildren."

After they parked directly in front of the coffee shop, Maddie got out of the truck. A few people walking down the street called out to Lincoln, and he greeted everyone with a wave. Of course, there were stares in her direction…all of them seemed friendly, but this was a town where everyone knew everyone else's business. She could imagine she was the talk of the town right now.

Once inside, Delia came bustling out of the kitchen.

"Maddie! Nice to see you again. And you, Lincoln. How are you? Do you need a menu?"

Lincoln replied, "I'm all set. I'm going to have a cheeseburger basket with fries. Maddie?"

Maddie looked at the wall behind the counter where the day's specials were posted. "You probably can't make this, but I really have a craving for a Maine lobster roll. I haven't had one in ages, but it's not a problem if you can't." Grinning at Delia, she added, "Sorry. It's Lincoln's fault. He told me you could make anything, even if it wasn't on the menu."

Delia returned the smile. "That is mostly true. You are in luck. I got some lobsters in this morning I could not refuse. Do you want to make your order a basket and have some fries or onion rings with it? And what would you like for drinks?"

"Onion rings sound great and I'll have a coffee, if you don't mind."

"Lincoln, coffee for you, too? Or would you rather have a Coke?"

"Coffee is great," he replied, and Delia returned quickly to the kitchen. To Maddie, he said, "You met Delia?"

"Yeah. The day I came to the lawyer's office, I stopped in for coffee first."

Lincoln glanced at the door opening. "Speak of the devil. Sal, how are you?"

Sal sauntered over to their table and his eyes locked with Maddie's. "I'm good. How about you, Madelyn? Is everything going okay?"

Maddie was not sure what to say. No decision had been made yet. "Well, I am… I'm going to stick around this week, but I'd like to get to know Kyle better and learn more about the farm before I make any decision."

Sal's face became serious. "I understand, but I would like to have an answer soon, Maddie. The quicker we get a decision, the easier it will be to move on or get things going. I've already got the paperwork set up for you to sign, if that's what you choose. Now, if you will excuse me, I have to fill this stomach so I can get some work done. See you soon, Maddie?"

"You certainly will and thank you!" Maddie stood up and shook his hand. When she sat down, though, her thoughts turned to dismay. Was she doing the right thing in even thinking about it? She had not even been there for the full weekend. How could she make an educated decision so quickly? How could she even think about becoming Kyle's guardian when she didn't even know him?

Lincoln reached over and grabbed her hand in his own. "It's okay. It's scary to jump from one life into another, but you've got this. I promise."

Maddie stared at their hands on the table. "How do you know that? What if Kyle decides he doesn't like me or want anything to do with me? How can I do a job I know nothing about?"

Maddie felt his fingers close around hers tighter. "Kyle already likes you. He's worried about the same thing. As for the job of running the farm, I'll be there to help you, and so will Kyle. I won't leave you in the lurch."

"Really? You'll stick around to help if I decide to do this?"

Lincoln let go of her hand and leaned back in his chair. "Of course I will. I do have to go back to my job soon, but for the time being, I'm yours."

Mine? If only you were mine. Maddie scolded herself for letting her thoughts stray away from what was important. She was obviously attracted to Lincoln. What girl wouldn't be? But right now, Kyle was the most important thing. Then there was the farm. She would need Lincoln's help. She did not need to mess that up because she could not keep her mind from going astray.

"Thank you. That means a lot. I really need to figure out what I'm going to do. I know Sal is frustrated with me—you probably are, too. I'm frustrated with me, too."

"It's going to be alright. I promise."

At that moment, Delia came out carrying their trays. Digging into the lobster roll, Maddie could only groan with delight. This place would make living in Maine worth it. *If* she moved to Maine.

After lunch was finished and Delia sent them off with a smile, Lincoln directed her across the street to the small market where Kyle worked. Ray's Market, according to the sign out front, sold everything from groceries and clothing to appliances and wedding dresses. Stifling a laugh, she could imagine what some of her co-workers would think of it.

Working at the ad agency required her to work with some of the top businesses in the Boston area. She dealt directly with some of them and, while she seemed to be well-liked by them, she did not often reciprocate those feelings. Many of them walked around like they were better than everyone else, and they often treated the staff rudely.

Even she had been treated that way when she was first starting out.

Would she miss her work? Maybe a little bit, but she really had only gone into the business because she liked challenges. This time around, the challenge seemed to have found her.

Once they stepped foot into the market, Lincoln steered her in the direction of the office after pointing out Kyle as he bagged a customer's order. A smile was on his face as he grabbed items coming down the conveyor belt. *At least he seems to love his job*, Maddie thought.

The door to the office was open and Lincoln leaned in. "You got a minute Ray?"

"Absolutely. What can I do for you, Lincoln? Kyle seems to be doing good."

"I wanted to introduce you to his cousin, Maddie. Maddie may be coming to live with Kyle at the farm and, eventually…if she stays on…she will be the one driving him back and forth to work. I wanted to give you both a chance to meet."

Maddie reached out to shake Ray's hand. "It's so nice to meet you. Kyle looks happy here."

Ray nodded his head. "He's a good young man. A couple of people gave their condolences about Daisy and Kyle nodded, said thank you, and went right back to work. It's just how he's handling things, I guess. But, if you ever need anything, let me know. Me and Kyle are good."

"Well, I appreciate that. And the same goes for you. If anything comes up, please don't hesitate to let me know."

After the introduction to Ray, Maddie asked Lincoln for a tour of the market. Mostly, she wanted to see how things were set up where they could sell wedding dresses. Not that she was interested. But it was something you didn't see every day. At least not in Boston.

When Lincoln walked her down to the back of the store, he pointed to a set of stairs leading up to the second floor. "Clothing and just about everything else is up there that isn't groceries or tools."

"Do you mind if I look?" she quickly asked. "I can meet you down here in a couple of minutes."

"Take your time. Kyle doesn't punch out for another fifteen. I've got to pick up a few things anyway."

Upstairs, Maddie could not believe it. Rack after rack held clothing of every size. Signs hung from above stated Girls, Boys, Women, and Men. A big sign in the back hung down that simply said, Wedding Apparel.

Walking around through the crowded racks, Maddie came across a section for shoes. Looking through the boots, she realized she had nothing at home that would last under the farm chores she was about to take on. Grabbing a pair of tan work boots in her size, she quickly tried them on and stood up. These were a must-have and soon she was grabbing a few more pairs of jeans and adding them to her growing pile.

When she walked downstairs again, her arms were full of things she decided she needed. Kyle seemed happy to see her and carefully inspected each item before it was placed inside the brown paper bag.

"Nice boots, Maddie," he said.

"Thanks, Kyle. Maybe they'll help me do better with the chores." She knew she had said the right thing when a grin broke out on his face.

Lincoln stepped up and said, "Time to clock out, Kyle."

Maddie followed Lincoln out to the truck and waited for Kyle with him. When he came out, he still had the smile on his face. But then the most serious look took over and he told her, "I call shotgun. That means you got to sit in the middle."

Laughing, Maddie climbed in the truck and quickly became somber when she realized what a tight fit it would be. When Lincoln and Kyle got in, she found herself pressed up against Lincoln. Feeling a little uncomfortable, she squirmed in her seat until Kyle spoke up. "Maddie, you got to sit still."

If she had not glanced at Lincoln, she would have missed the little grin that passed across his features. *What have you gotten yourself into, Madelyn Presley Jones? Just pay attention to the road ahead of you*, was all she could think.

Chapter Nine

Monday morning, Maddie listened to the sound of the rooster crowing and covered her head with the pillow. She was not a morning person, especially after a night of tossing and turning. Different scenarios had flown out of her head all night long. What if Kyle decided he did not want her as a guardian? What would happen if she ran the farm into the ground? What if Lincoln left her high and dry?

Lincoln was what was holding everything together. In three days, she had found out the aunt she had thought dead for twenty years had been alive the whole time. She found out her aunt adopted a baby with special needs, and she was now supposed to be his caregiver and the owner of a farm. A farm! If it weren't for Lincoln, she might have high-tailed it out of there the first day.

The whole idea of needing somebody was foreign to her. The early death of her family members made her rely on nobody but herself. Now, here she was, stuck in Maine and completely reliant on someone she barely knew.

Deciding she may as well get up and get a start to the day, Maddie got dressed and, before going into the bathroom, grabbed a piece of paper and wrote the words BATHROOM IS OCCUPIED on it before taping it to the door. Living in this house with one bathroom was not going to work, especially if the door to the only bathroom did not have a lock. She wondered how Kyle would do if she stayed and decided to renovate.

Finding the kitchen empty, Maggie rummaged through the cupboards until she found the coffee and made a full pot. She would need as much caffeine as possible if she planned on getting anything done today. She knew she would need to make a quick trip to the funeral parlor to provide them with the dress she had picked out for her Aunt Daisy and make sure everything was all set with the funeral. It would be tough, but much better if she went by herself.

Kyle was not working today, so he and Lincoln were planning on repairing a couple of fences and making sure the animals were set. That left her alone for pretty much the rest of the day to get things done in the office. If she were staying, she needed to get organized. Even if she left, she could not leave it looking the way it did.

After listening for sounds from upstairs and hearing nothing, Maddie glanced at the clock. Only quarter to six. She should be able to get in an hour of work in the office before anyone came downstairs, and she grabbed a cup of coffee to take with her. Before getting to the office, however, she had four dogs surrounding her.

"You all probably want to go out, huh? Follow me. I'll just drink my coffee on the porch."

As soon as she opened the door, all four trotted out to the yard. Within minutes, all were back on the porch and staring at her. The smallest of them, Peaches, pawed at her legs. "Oh Peaches. Come up here," she whispered. As she settled onto her lap, Peaches let out a long growl. "I know exactly how you feel, sweetie. Life has sure thrown us some curve balls, huh?"

Looking around at her surroundings, Maddie couldn't help but smile. The only way to describe the morning was peaceful. The sun was shining, and she could hear the distant sounds of the animals in the barn. She wished she knew what needed to be done, so she could get the morning chores started. That thought made her snicker. The idea that she could be a farm girl made her feel more peaceful. Perhaps this whole thing was meant to be?

At the sound of the door opening, Maddie turned to see Lincoln coming out the door holding his own cup of coffee.

"Thanks for making coffee this morning. I see you've made a friend," he said, nodding toward Peaches lying in her lap.

"I guess I have. Kyle said she hasn't been eating. Maybe this is what she needs. I'll try taking her in the office with me this morning and give her a little attention. Hopefully, she'll eat. She feels so thin," she replied.

As if she knew they were talking about her, Peaches looked up at Maddie and then her little tongue reached out and lapped at her hand.

Lincoln nodded. "This dog was definitely Daisy's dog. Not quite the same as Mutley is with Kyle, but Daisy was her person. Maybe she'll attach herself to you? That's probably what she needs. Well, I am going to get breakfast ready. Anything you want special?"

"Um, no, but I guess I should learn what Kyle likes. Now is as good a time as any," Maddie said as she got up, making sure to cradle Peaches in her arms.

After watching and helping Lincoln get the morning chores done inside the house and trying to learn how to make morning easy for Kyle, Maddie grabbed another cup of coffee, picked up Peaches and finally made it into the office. It was only eight o'clock in the morning, but she felt like she was running behind.

Sitting down at the desk after placing Peaches on a blanket close by, she started sorting through the paperwork on the desk. There seemed to be no rhyme or reason for anything. Maddie picked out at least ten magazines from the pile and put them to the side. Sales flyers and grocery lists were thrown into the trash bin under the desk. Anything she was not sure of, she put in another pile to sort through afterward.

Picking up a file on the bottom of the stack, Maddie let out a little squeal. This was exactly what she had been looking for. Her excitement quickly turned sour, however, when she saw what it was. Inside was a contract with Blue Market Boys. From what she could tell, Daisy had not signed it yet. Or perhaps the signed contract had been mislaid in another pile? She could only hope it was the former.

The Blue Market Boys was the name of the firm Anthony and James Martinelli formed right out of college. She knew that because she had worked on a couple of ad campaigns for them. They were rude, pretentious, and condescending. She could only hope Daisy had not signed anything.

Sadly, she knew how they worked. Glancing through the contract, she could see they had not changed. As part of the contract they had drawn up for Daisy, there was a stipulation that all recipes used by her would become their property after one year. In other words, they would keep the recipes and throw her out the door. Maddie slammed the file on the desk and took a deep breath.

Standing up, she stretched, and her eyes fell on the calendar on the back of the door. Walking over to it, she glanced at the date and groaned. Seriously? Today was the day the Martinelli brothers were coming. She had forgotten all about it. She doubted very much they had heard about the death of her aunt. The only thing she could do was prepare, and she only had an hour to do it.

Running out of the office, she flew upstairs only to stop at the middle of the steps. Why was she worried about what she was wearing? This was not a fancy-schmancy meeting in Boston. They were coming here to the farm. No way was she changing out of her comfortable jeans, tee-shirt, and work boots.

Instead, she very carefully cleaned up the kitchen and the table in case they accepted a cup of coffee. She doubted they would come further than the porch after what she had to say. Time would tell.

At exactly nine-thirty, a long, black limo pulled into the yard. Maddie was on the porch and snickered. They could not even come to coastal Maine without trying to make themselves look like bigshots.

As soon as the back door opened, Maddie stepped off the porch. Both Anthony and James were there, which did not surprise her. One rarely was without the other. When they saw her, they obviously did not recognize her from the ad agency.

"Good morning. We are here to see Daisy. Would you please let her know we are here?"

"Sorry, guys. Daisy died last week. I just found out about this meeting. Otherwise, I would have called you."

Each of them held a stricken look on their face. "What do you mean? Died? Daisy? Daisy Carr?" Anthony asked with panic in his voice.

"Yes. Unfortunately, my aunt passed away. I did see a copy of the contract you sent her. I am assuming this is why you are here today. To see if she signed?" Maddie watched them and noticed the look exchanged between them.

"Yes, we are here to pick up the signed contract. Of course, the contract is still binding, regardless of her death," James stated.

"Sorry to tell you this, but she didn't sign." Maddie crossed her arms over her chest, waiting for them to respond.

"Didn't sign? She told us she signed it last week. You must not have the right copy. I am almost sure she faxed us a copy. We came here to clear things up and pick up the original."

Maddie could not stop herself and laughed. "Really? I'm sorry, but Daisy did not fax you a copy of the contract. Everything to do with Blue Market Boys is in one file. That's it, boys."

Both James and Anthony looked at her in surprise and then disgust.

"And whom might you be?" Anthony asked.

"I'm Madelyn Jones. I have worked with Wendy on a few of your accounts in the past. I came up here from Boston to help settle my aunt's estate. Quite frankly, I am surprised to find you this far away from the city," she retorted.

James laughed and held out his hand. "Well, it's good to see you again, Madelyn. I…uh…didn't recognize you in this atmosphere." His eyes roamed up and down, and he added, "Or in this attire. Well, I am glad you are here. We can get a new contract sent to you immediately with the proper information and whoever is now in charge of this place and keep the deal going. It won't take long at all."

Maddie ignored the hand in front of her. "Sorry. This business deal is not going to happen. The farm belongs to me now. I read the contract and can see how after a year you would have swindled my aunt out of her recipes and left her hanging with the few dollars you promised her. I am taking over the farm now and, I can tell you this. There is no contract between Dandelion Farms and Blue Market Boys and there never will be. Please don't waste your time on this anymore."

***

As the limo turned around and started back out the driveway, Maddie turned around to discover Lincoln right behind her.

"Was that about what I think it was?" he asked with a scowl on his face.

Maddie nodded. "It was. I worked with those bozos before in Boston. The contract they set up for Aunt Daisy would have left her high and dry after a year. It was not even worth negotiating with them for a better contract. The last entry in Aunt Daisy's journal talked about it like it was her lifelong dream. I feel horrible, but this route was not the way to go. I only hope Kyle understands."

"I am sure Kyle will be fine. I am glad you were here. You obviously know what you're doing." With a smile on his face, he added, "You are going to do just fine running this farm."

"Lincoln, I haven't decided I'm staying. I feel…horrible. If I choose to stay, I am going to be taking over Aunt Daisy's plan to get her products to the larger public. I know it's what she wanted, but I don't know if I'm the person to do that. What do I know about making jellies? For that matter, how do you make jelly?"

Lincoln steered her in the direction of the porch. "Relax. I only meant if you do make the decision to stay, I have no doubt the farm and business will do fine under your expertise. Kyle is out in the barn cleaning up. I've got to get back with him. Is there anything you need from either one of us?"

"No, I'm good. I am going to run down to the funeral home to make sure things are all set. After that, I'll probably be back in the office to try to get a handle on what Aunt Daisy was doing and what her plans were."

"Sounds good. I was thinking of lasagna for supper if that's okay with you. I figure about six?" he asked.

Maddie's eyes widened. "You actually cook? I mean, I know you've been making lunch and stuff, but lasagna? Sounds good to me."

"My mother made sure I could cook. Told me that to lure good women in, I needed to learn," he said with a gleam in his eyes.

Laughing the whole way, Maddie hurried upstairs to grab the outfit for the funeral home and her purse. Before leaving, she made sure to go back into the office to say goodbye to Peaches who was right where she left her. The little dog whimpered when Maddie praised her for eating the breakfast she had left in the dish beside her bed. "You're a good girl, Peaches. I know you miss your person, but eating is going to help you get through it." After a kiss on the top of the dog's head, she left the office, leaving the door ajar so the little dog could get out if she wanted.

Two hours later, she was pulling back in the driveway, feeling overwhelmed. The funeral home visit had not gone as planned. Aunt Daisy had planned her funeral two years prior to her death. She had even picked out the outfit for the funeral and the music she wanted played. What Maddie had not counted on was the director taking her in to view her aunt. She had not seen her in twenty years and suddenly there she was.

Aunt Daisy's hair, once long and auburn, was now speckled with gray and kept in a short bob. Her once youthful face was now lined and aged. Her beauty still stood out, regardless. Phoenix had once told her she looked like her aunt and now that Maddie had grown up, she could see it herself. Reaching out, Maddie placed her hand on top of Daisy's.

Noticing what her Aunt Daisy was wearing, she allowed herself to smile. One thing about her aunt that had not changed over the years was not caring what others thought. Daisy was dressed the way she always dressed. A long-sleeved shirt with her overalls. On her feet were a pair of rain boots.

Emotions that had been bottled up for years spewed forth and Maddie found herself trembling. This was the one woman she had looked up to and wanted to be like. This was the woman who made her feel like she was truly special. When she had lost her twenty years ago, she had been devastated. Her parents did not like to talk about her, so through the years, Maddie learned not to speak her name or she would face the glares from both her parents. Now, here she was in front of her, but in body only.

Maddie reached out and carefully touched her aunt's hand. "I'm so sorry, Aunt Daisy. I thought you were gone years ago. If only I had known. I remember a few years back, I thought about driving up here to check out the farm, but I couldn't do it. I knew it wouldn't be the same without you and now here I am. It's not the same. But I will promise you this. I will make sure Kyle is taken care of, whether I stay here or not. I won't disappear out of his life even if I don't stay. I wish I could tell you I am going to accept your inheritance, but…I can't. Not yet. I never forgot you, Aunt Daisy and I never will," she whispered.

After leaving the funeral home in tears, Maddie took a few moments in the parking lot. Seeing Aunt Daisy had brought up so many memories of the woman who once meant the world to her. Now she was gone, and what more could she do but accept the inheritance? Kyle was not only Daisy's son. He was her cousin. Knowing she had to do this was one thing. Carrying out her aunt's wishes would be a lot tougher.

As she drove to Sal's office, Maddie's knuckles turned white. Was she jumping into this decision? She had never been the type to make rash decisions, and she knew she was making it based on emotions only. There was no way she could turn the offer down after seeing her Aunt Daisy.

At Sal's office, she was ushered right in. "I'm so glad you came to the decision to stay with Kyle. He's really a good kid. The community here loves him. They will all be relieved to know a relative is going to take care of him. All I need you to do is sign the paperwork I have here, and then we will get the deed and all that goes with it signed over to your name, including her bank accounts. There is a trust set up for Kyle, and I will have your name added to that, as well. You certainly don't have to worry about money now. Daisy made sure Kyle would be set for life."

Maddie signed the paperwork and asked, "Did my aunt ever come to you about a contract with the Blue Market Brothers?"

"No, she didn't. Why?" he asked.

"I guess it doesn't really matter now, but they had interest in her jelly and wine recipes. I know she had wanted to expand what she offered."

Sal laughed. "She did. Evidently having her stuff in the local stores wasn't enough for her. Daisy had dreams, I would say. She never came to me about any contracts, though. Do you need help with the contract?"

"No. There is no contract. I was familiar with the company and I sent them packing. I am just hoping I can do the farm and Kyle justice. I definitely have some big shoes to fill," Maddie replied.

"I am sure you will do just fine. Daisy was a good woman. I've known her for years, which is why I was so surprised when she used someone else as an attorney when she adopted Kyle," he told her in a lowered voice.

"I don't know, but I'm glad I was on the list to be Kyle's guardian. I'm hopeful our relationship will get better. So far, things are…well, not great, but not bad, either."

"It will. Kyle is a fine young man. Well, I will see you tomorrow at the funeral. I don't mean to rush you off, but I have a date with the golf course later today and I can't go until I get this stuff done. Remember, if you work hard, you must play hard, too," he said as he stood up.

"Absolutely. I'll see you tomorrow then."

Work hard was something she had down. It was the playing hard thing she needed to practice. Driving back to the farm, her home now, all she could think about was the promise she had made to her aunt and how she could make it work. Now, sitting in her car staring at the house in front of her, all she wanted to do was cry. But with Kyle watching her from the porch, she took a deep breath and opened the car door.

***

Breathing in through her nose and out through her mouth, Maddie opened the car door to greet Kyle with a smile. "Sorry I took so long, Kyle."

Kyle grinned. "We got the chores done, but we still have to do them tonight. Do you want to help if I promise not to laugh?"

Maddie's smile widened. "I promise to help, and you can even laugh if I do something silly."

Kyle clapped his hands and jumped up and down. "It's a deal," he squealed as Lincoln came out the front door.

"What did I miss?" he asked.

"Maddie said she'll help with the chores tonight. She said I can laugh if she does something silly." With that said, Kyle took off running for the barn, leaving Maddie and Lincoln alone.

"Well, you certainly made him happy. How did today go?" he asked.

Maddie's smile disappeared. Tears welled up in her eyes. "I saw my Aunt Daisy at the funeral home. I can't believe how old she looked. She used to be so…vibrant…so full of energy. I don't think the last twenty-years was easy on her. I know she had a heart attack, but…still. Twenty-years ago she was something else."

Lincoln placed his hand on her arm. "The last twenty years might have been hard, but I can guarantee you that she enjoyed every minute of it. She was still vibrant and full of energy. The woman didn't know how to relax, which probably didn't help her heart."

Wiping at her eyes, Maddie looked down at her feet. "You're right. I know she didn't regret her life with Kyle or the life she created for herself on this farm. Now I've got to find a way to let it live on." Pausing, Maddie looked around at the farm and back to Lincoln. "This is all mine now, Lincoln. I signed the paperwork in Sal's office after I left the funeral home," she whispered.

Lincoln let out a whoop and pulled her into his arms. "Oh, Maddie! You've made me a happy man today. Congratulations, Maddie."

Maddie sunk into Lincoln's arms. It had been so long since she had been in a man's arms. "Thank you. I'm hoping I did the right thing."

Lincoln unwound his arms from around her and stepped back. "You did the right thing. Now, you have to find a way to make it yours. What would Daisy want? You following her dream or you following your own?"

"What do you mean?"

"Daisy wouldn't want you to only do everything she had planned. She would have wanted you to make this place yours…to create a new dream for yourself that could coincide with what is best for you and Kyle."

Maddie looked toward the barn where Kyle was in deep conversation with Marvin or Madelyn. She could not remember which donkey was which, but it looked as though the donkey was actively listening as its ears and tail twitched. A slight breeze drifted around her and the smell of salt was in the air. Closing her eyes, Maddie could almost feel her aunt standing beside her. When she opened them, she found Lincoln looking at her with a concerned expression.

"I'm okay. Just taking it all in, I guess. Look at Kyle. He obviously loves this place. I have made the decision, signed the papers, and now, I guess I have to talk to him about it. Maybe tonight after supper. The biggest hurdle is going to be getting through the funeral tomorrow. Does Kyle know what to expect?"

"I've talked to him a little bit about funerals, but no matter what, it's going to be one of the most difficult moments in his life. Daisy had things planned, thankfully, but I do not think she thought the whole open-casket thing through. I'm not sure how Kyle will react to seeing her." Lincoln turned to look at Kyle who was now playing tag with the donkeys.

"I hadn't seen her in twenty years and it just about killed me. I can't imagine what it will be like for him."

Maddie thought a moment before asking, "Could we change it to a closed casket? Or somehow keep him from seeing her?"

Lincoln shook his head. "No, we can't. And as much as I want to protect him from the pain, we have to remember these were Daisy's wishes. She even planned out the get-together afterward at the church. Paid for the catering, too."

Maddie looked at Lincoln. The poor man was worried sick about Kyle and she could see it on his face. Tomorrow was going to be a rough day. The only thing she could do was to try to keep herself together. Her stomach in knots, she looked into Lincoln's eyes. "I'll talk to him some more tonight after the chores are done."

The lasagna supper Lincoln made had Maddie moaning in delight. "You really should give up your job and work as a chef. This is better than some of the finer restaurants in Boston."

Kyle shoveled a bite in his mouth and mumbled, "It's good, Lincoln."

Lincoln laughed. "I grew up in restaurants. My father was a chef. I like to cook, but not every day."

"Well, you definitely got some of his abilities. I've been cooking since my teens and I can't make anything that tastes like this," Maddie stated and then lifted the fork to her mouth.

Kyle let out a burp and covered his mouth, his eyes wide. Maddie could not help but laugh. "You know, in China, a belch is considered a compliment."

Laughter from Kyle and Lincoln made Maddie smile even wider. Thankfully, the mood lasted throughout the evening chores. Kyle kept his eye on her the whole time and, only once, did she give him cause to laugh. When Elsa and Anna were brought into their stall, the smallest one, Elsa got too close and caused Maddie to trip over her. Kyle let out a giggle and Maddie gave him a thumbs up. His mood was great until Maddie sat down with him after coming in for the night.

"Kyle, I did sign papers today to become your guardian. On Wednesday morning, I'm going to drive to Boston to have my stuff packed up and shipped here. Then I'll be here all the time. Okay?."

Kyle nodded his head while petting Mutley.

"I don't know a lot about the farm, but I'm really hoping you and Lincoln can teach me everything I need to know. First, however, we have to get through tomorrow. Do you understand what a funeral is?" Maddie asked and reached her hand toward his knee. Kyle pulled his leg back.

"I know what a funeral is, Maddie. I'm not stupid." It was the first time Maddy had ever noticed an edge to his voice, and it unsettled her.

"I know you're not stupid, Kyle. I want to make sure you're prepared. Funerals are tough. My sister's funeral was extremely hard on me. I was only eleven years old."

Kyle's eyes narrowed. "Your sister died?"

Maddie nodded. "So did my mother and my father. Their funerals were very difficult, too. I thought if you had any questions, I could answer them for you."

Kyle reached out and placed his hand in hers. "I'm sorry everyone died, Maddie."

"Me, too," she whispered. "Tomorrow is going to be hard, but I want you to remember both Lincoln and I will be right there by your side."

"I know," Kyle replied. She watched as he stood up and left the room, with Mutley right on his heels.

Lincoln peered in from the doorway. "Good job. That was a tough conversation to have, but both of you handled it well. I think you and Kyle are going to be just fine."

Maddie picked at a hangnail. A week ago, her hands had looked polished and beautiful. In less than a week, her hands were in desperate need of a manicure. But what would be the point? Within a few days, they would be back to looking like they did now.

Looking at Lincoln, she whispered, "I'm scared. What if I'm not cut out for this? What if I can't do it? What if I run this place into the ground or what if Kyle suddenly hates me?"

Lincoln leaned his face closer to hers. "It's normal to feel scared when you are faced with something like this. This is all new, but I can tell you what I know. Kyle will never hate you. You know how I know that? Because I know Kyle. Give it time. All of it. Nothing that is worth anything is going to come easy. Be prepared to take a few steps forward and then a few steps back. It happens. But no matter what does happen, I'll be here to help if you need it. So will everyone else."

"Everyone else?"

"Everyone that knew Daisy and knows Kyle. I guarantee it."

Maddie did not know what to say and continued to pick at her nails. She only wished tomorrow was a hurdle she had already gotten over.

Chapter Ten

Maddie sat in the front row of the church beside Kyle. Lincoln sat on the other side of him. In a few moments, the pastor would ask if anyone wanted to say something about her Aunt Daisy. As much as Maddie loved her aunt, she had not seen her in twenty years. She was not sure how many people at the service knew that, but how could she explain her absence? The truth? Not going to happen.

As soon as the words came out of the pastor's mouth, Maddie's breath caught in her throat. Kyle stood up beside her and shuffled to the podium. His eyes never looked at the casket in the front. Turning her head, she caught Lincoln's surprised expression. They both watched in shock as Kyle took his place and started to speak.

"My mum was a good mother. She taught me everything I know about farming. She loved animals almost as much as me. She loved to talk. But most of all, she loved me. And I loved her. I still do. Now I got my cousin Maddie. It's not the same without Mum. But Lincoln told me that Mum will always be with me. I just can't see her." Kyle looked at the casket in front. "I know. She's right there, but she's not. That's just her body that God gave her. It's not her anymore."

Kyle's eyes roamed through the crowded room and rested on Maddie. "Maddie's right there," he said, and pointed to her. "She don't know how to do a lot, but I guess I can teach her."

A few giggles erupted from the crowd and Maddie wiped at her tears. Kyle motioned for her to come up and Maddie breathed in deep. The last thing she wanted to do was stand up in a crowd of people she did not know, but at this point, she had no choice.

It wasn't until she was standing by Kyle's side and holding his hand that the words came to her. "Thank you, Kyle. Sadly, my aunt and I lost touch over the last twenty years, but that was not due to my not loving her. My Aunt Daisy, even though she was only a part of the first nine years of my life, helped to shape me into who I am today. I have so many great memories of my time spent here in Cove's Port with her. As sad as I am to say my Aunt Daisy is gone, I am happy I get to make new memories with Kyle."

Maddie, still holding onto Kyle's hand, led him down from the podium and back into their seats. Keeping her eyes down, she leaned toward Kyle, whispering, "You did a great job, Kyle. Your mother would be proud."

Kyle squeezed her hand. She was not sure what she was expecting, but it was not Kyle acting more together than she was. From where she sat, Kyle was acting like an adult. Deep down, though, she knew he was hurting inside. She had been through it herself. The tears would come later followed by anger. Then, if he was lucky, he would accept his mother's death and move on with his life. Like she had. Or had not, according to Kyra.

Kyra was always at her that she was afraid to get too close to anyone because everyone she loved had died. Yeah, maybe she did put people at arm's length, but she had her reasons. Fear of getting hurt? No. It was more the idea that most people just did not measure up to what she demanded from them.

As for Kyra, there was no arguing the point with her. Once she had an idea in her head, she refused to consider anything else. For the last eight years Kyra had been pushing Maddie to forge other relationships. Well, now that this sudden change had brought Kyle and Lincoln into her life, she hoped Kyra would back off on social life.

Kyle stood up, pulling Maddie with him. The service was over, and in a few minutes, they would be expected to go to the church basement. Daisy had preplanned everything, including catering the event. The basement was packed when they arrived downstairs, and she believed Kyle was probably more prepared for this than she was. Sure, she made sure he was prepared for it, but she should have given herself a talk before today.

When they walked in, Maddie's chest tightened. The whole town and probably some from the surrounding towns were there. She knew Daisy was all about community, but she had no idea this many would show up. Within seconds of walking in, Kyle had left her and Lincoln. She watched as people reached out to him and he would nod and even accept a hug.

"Lincoln, I was so wrong about how Kyle would handle this," she whispered.

Lincoln kept his eyes on Kyle. "Better than I expected, but don't be surprised if he gets overwhelmed."

A hand reached out and touched her arm from the side, and Maddie turned to find an elderly woman with familiar eyes.

"Maddie, you probably don't remember me, but I used to spend some time with you when you were a little one. Phyllis Drummond. I live just a few miles down the road."

"Mrs. Drummond, yes, I remember. Aunt Daisy used to bring me to your house, and you would feed me all those scrumptious cookies. It's so good to see you." The last time she had visited, she had left one of the young kittens she had rescued, and bottle-fed. Mrs. Drummond had promised to bottle-feed it on the same schedule she and her aunt had set up. "I remember you adopted one of the kittens Aunt Daisy and I raised."

"Rosco, yes. You won't believe this, but he turned twenty this year. Not doing so well now, but he's led a long and happy life."

"He's still alive? Oh my gosh. You don't know how happy that makes me." Maddie took Mrs. Drummond's hand and squeezed. "You made my day."

"Please, Maddie. Call me Phyllis. I would love it if you could stop by sometime soon. I could even make some cookies for old time's sake. We can catch up on the last twenty years. And, honestly, I've been pretty darned lonely since Daisy passed. She stopped in at least three times a week, even if it was for only five minutes. She had such a kind heart." Phyllis sniffled. "Sorry, Maddie. I don't mean to break down. If you need anything at all, you let me know."

Maddie kept her eyes on Phyllis as she wandered across the room to the food table. It only took a second for someone else to introduce themselves to her and soon she was flooded with memories of times in Cove's Port. Every single person who came up to her had wonderful things to say about Daisy, offer their condolences, and, of course, offering assistance with the farm and Kyle. Not one person asked why she had not been to see her aunt in twenty years. Not one. That was until Mr. Pearson arrived. As the owner of the local newspaper, Mr. Pearson liked to know what was going on.

"Young lady, I'm sure you don't remember me, but you used to come to the newspaper to place ads for whatever Daisy decided to sell. Mr. Charles Pearson. I own the newspaper. I realize Daisy's death brought you back to Cove's Port, but if you don't mind my asking, what kept you away so long?"

"I, um…" Maddie stumbled on her words. "It's a long story."

"Well, I'm happy to hear it whenever you are ready. Daisy was a big part of this place. I hope you're considering stepping up into some of the roles she filled around here."

The hair on the back of her neck stood up and goosebumps appeared down her bare arms. She was not sure if she was going to like Mr. Pearson or not. He seemed a little pushy and seemed to believe because he had met her before he could say what was on his mind. "Well, Mr. Pearson, I can assure you I am stepping into Daisy's biggest role. Thank you. Now, if you will excuse me, I have to check on Kyle."

Turning to walk away, she found Lincoln right beside her.

"Don't let Charles get to you. He is like that with everyone. Wants to know what's going on and why. It's the reporter in him. Always looking for a story," he said, steering her further away from the crowd to where Kyle was sitting at a table eating with a few people around his own age.

"Yeah. He was a little unnerving," she said. "I wasn't exactly sure what to say."

"Don't worry about it. Charles is a good guy. I'm sure he meant well. So, what time are you leaving for Boston?"

Maddie groaned. "As early as I can. I'm going to hire someone to come in and pack and ship, but I need to get my personal items. I also need to tell my boss I won't be back. I'm hoping I will be back before supper, but don't count on it."

"Please don't feel you have to rush back. I've got things for now. Do what you have to do, but don't hurry. Okay?"

Maddie noticed the concern on his face, and felt her face grow warm. It had been a long time since anyone worried about her. And the fact that it was coming from Lincoln made it all that much better.

"Maddie, I'm going outside with Matt and Tony. We're going to play catch," Kyle interrupted.

"Who are Matt and Tony?" Maddie had not met any of Kyle's friends yet.

"Matt and Tony Wallace graduated from high school with Kyle. Just stay right around the backyard, Kyle.

I'm sure a lot of people want to see you before they leave," Lincoln stated.

Maddie watched Kyle hurry to the door and turned to Lincoln. "Should he leave? I mean…this is his mother's funeral."

"He's fine. I'm not sure what funerals are like in the city, but here in Cove's Port, it's not just a gathering. It's more like…well, a party," Lincoln replied. "As you can see, your aunt wanted a gathering with good food and good people. This will give Kyle a chance to hang with some of his friends, too. Matt and Tony are twins, and they've been friends with Kyle since kindergarten. You see, Kyle was not put in any special classes. Oh, he needed some help with reading and writing at the beginning, but he was not singled out because he was different than his classmates. He has always been included, which is how it should be."

Maddie turned and looked at the people around her. Many were standing with plates in their hands, eating while they talked with friends, family, and neighbors. Both her parents' funerals had been small in attendance and nothing at all like this. Phoenix's funeral had been huge, but mostly because it had been held in the school's auditorium and the whole student body had gathered to pay their respects.

"How are you doing, Maddie?" Delia asked as she came up and stood beside her.

"I'm doing okay. I didn't expect so many people. Thank you for coming,"

Delia put her hand on Maddie's arm. "I wouldn't miss it. Daisy was a wonderful person. She was a big help to me when my girls were younger. If my in-laws couldn't watch them, Daisy would watch them for me. It was never more than a few hours, but believe me, they could be a handful.”

“How old are your girls?” Maddie couldn’t help but feel a little jealousy toward them.

“Sixteen and fourteen. Just close enough that all they do is fight. They fight about clothes, boys, and any other thing they can think of. Do you have any siblings?”

Maddie nodded, and then shook her head. “Well, I did. My sister was almost six years older, but she passed away when I was twelve.”

Delia’s smile disappeared. “I’m sorry. I wouldn’t have asked…”

“No. It’s okay. Honestly, it was so long ago. I’m fine to talk about it. We did our share of fighting, though. Probably not about the same things as your girls, but we did argue.”

“Well, these two never stop.” Delia’s smile returned. “Where’s Kyle? I wanted to say hello to him before I leave.”

Maddie pointed to the door. “Kyle is out back playing catch with a couple of his friends.”

“Good for him. I’ll go out that way and see him. He’s a good kid. Remember, if you need anything at all, you can find me at the coffee shop.”

After Delia left, others started to come by to say goodbye to her before they left. Most offered to help her with the farm or Kyle. Whatever she needed. Whenever she needed it. She even had a couple offer up her sons to help her clean the pig’s pen. After seeing the pen, she actually wished she could remember their names. Cleaning out the pigs was not something she wanted to take on.

***

After Lincoln and Kyle came in from doing the nightly chores, Maddie sat on the front porch. This was going to be her life after tomorrow. Instead of hearing sirens at all hours of the night, she would be here, listening to the donkeys bray, the chickens cluck, and the geese honking. And she couldn't forget the peepers. Every night just before dark, the peepers would start. Occasionally, she would hear an owl in the distance, and last night, she had heard a sound she had never heard before. She had run in to grab Lincoln, who laughed, and told her it was a woodcock. He had then laughed and said, "City girl's gotta learn about the country."

Now, smiling, she listened to the woodcock calling out somewhere near the barn and grinned. This country thing definitely had its up sides.

Chapter Eleven

Maddie pulled into the driveway, breathing a deep feeling of relief. Her car was packed full of all the items she did not want broken in the transit and things she could use right now, including her laptop. Maybe now she could get things straightened out in the office and figure out what was going on.

The lights were on in the kitchen, and before she could even open the door, Kyle was on the porch.

"Maddie! Guess what? We got a puppy. I named him Dudley, but you can change it if you want. You like that name, though, right?" Kyle said, the excitement causing him to bounce around the porch.

"A puppy? Another dog?" Maddie asked. *Five weren't enough?* She silently chided herself for sounding like her mother.

"It's a stray. Lincoln thinks it's only a couple of months old. We found it on the side of the road. Lincoln said I could keep it."

Maddie did not know what to think. How could Lincoln tell Kyle he could keep it when he did not even check with her? This was not what she needed. Maddie grumbled, "Give me a minute, Kyle. I've got to unpack my car and get all this stuff into the house." She cringed when the smile disappeared from Kyle's face. She quickly added, "But first, I want to go see the puppy."

Kyle squealed and ran back into the house with Maddie following closely behind. In the living room, Kyle led her to a box where a tiny, black and white puppy slept on a blanket. She turned to Lincoln who was sitting on the couch between Bella and Lily. "This puppy was on the side of the road? The one you told him he could keep?"

Nodding his head, Lincoln said, "People are cruel. They don't fix their dogs and then throw out the puppies. I figured it would do Kyle some good."

Reaching down, Maddie picked up the puppy, who stretched and yawned. It felt like skin and bones. "Oh, sweetie. You poor thing. It's a good thing they found you."

Lincoln laughed. "I guess you've got a new dog."

"Evidently," she muttered. To Kyle she asked, "What kind do you think it is?" she asked.

"It's a terrier-mix. I think. We need to make an appointment at the vet. Mr. Keegan will tell us." Kyle stroked the puppy's head and smiled at Maddie.

"Yes. We'll do that tomorrow." Placing the puppy back in the box, she watched as it lay back down to go back to sleep. Turning around, she asked, "You boys want to help me unload my car?"

Kyle jumped up and ran out the door. Lincoln stood up and stretched. "Sure thing. Glad you made it back. I ordered Chinese tonight. I put yours in the fridge. All you got to do is warm it up."

"Thank you. It's been a long day," she said and then whispered, "Another puppy, Lincoln? I wish you would have asked me before telling Kyle he could keep it. Six dogs?"

Lincoln reached out and placed his hand on her arm. "It will be good for Kyle. You'll see. However, I promise to never make any decisions again with consulting you first. I was wrong."

Giving Lincoln a smile, Maddie stepped back and said, "Come on. My car is packed."

A few hours later, Maddie was exhausted, but she felt great her that things were put away. The computer was set up in the office, her clothes hung up in the closet and put away in the bureau, and personal items made her bedroom feel more like her own. What she would do with the rest of her stuff when the truck arrived, she had no idea.

When Maddie wandered back downstairs, Kyle was in his room, either playing with the puppy or sleeping. Looking through the cupboard, Maddie decided on her aunt's dandelion tea and had set the tea kettle on the stove when Lincoln came through the door.

"Tea?" she asked. "I'm trying my aunt's dandelion tea."

"No, but I would take some dandelion wine. You want some of that instead?"

"Wine? Dandelion wine?" Shutting off the burner on the stove, she turned to him. "I have got to try that. Have you had it before?"

Lincoln moved to the fridge and pulled out a bottle and grabbed two wine glasses from the cupboard. "Many times. Daisy didn't make this to sell, but she would give it away. I'm surprised you haven't had anyone knocking on the door yet to see if there's any left."

When Lincoln handed her the glass, she tipped it toward her and sniffed. "It smells like…I'm not sure. It smells almost earthy."

Lincoln took a sip of his and smiled. "Come on, now. None of that fancy stuff. Just take a sip."

A giggle escaped from her lips. Lincoln had an almost 'I dare you' look on his face and she was never one to escape a dare. Putting the glass to her lips, she tipped the glass to find herself pleasantly surprised. "Oh my God! This is good. I can't believe this is made from dandelions."

Lincoln grabbed the bottle and made his way into the living room. Bella and Lily were curled up on their couch and did not move an inch when Maddie sat between them. Lincoln sat in one of the chairs and placed the bottle in between them on the coffee table.

"Your aunt was one of a kind. She loved dandelions. I'm not sure of the significance of them, but dandelions were the main ingredient for a lot of her products."

"I'm not sure, but I can see her doing it. When I was a kid, we spent a lot of time outdoors and she loved cooking."

Maddie smiled, remembering some of the summers she had spent here on the farm. She and her aunt would spend a lot of time picking wildflowers and putting together bouquets to decorate the farmhouse. Many often went to friends and neighbors, including Carol at the coffee shop.

One day Maddie had put together a bouquet all on her own and had surprised her aunt with it. Most of the flowers in it had been dandelions. Her aunt had told her she loved it and said dandelions were her favorite. *"They're the strongest flower out there, Madelyn. Most people hate them and call them a weed. They are not a weed...not in my eyes. They persevere, no matter what. That's a good trait to have."*

Surveying the room, Maddie knew this really was the only place she felt at home. She still could not believe this place was hers and almost laughed at the thought. Her adulthood had changed her. And not necessarily for the better.

Lincoln refilled her glass with wine and leaned back in his chair. *He really is a good-looking guy*, Maddie thought to herself. Maddie in Boston probably would not have given him a second look. However, Maddie on the farm was a whole different story.

Looking over at Lincoln, she asked, "Why do you care so much?"

"Why not?" he asked her. "What's wrong with going through life caring about the people around you?"

Maddie groaned. "Don't answer a question with a question."

"It wasn't intentional but think about it. If you do not care about other people, who is going to care about you?"

What was he getting at? Did he think she did not care about anyone? Or did he think no one cared about her? That was not the case at all. She cared. She and Kyra had been friends since they met in first grade. How many people could say they were still best friends with someone they met when they were so young? So, what if she didn't have many other close? Her family was gone. Except for Kyle, and she hadn't even known about him until last week.

"I get what you are saying, but what I was asking was why do you care so much about Kyle and what happens to him? Are you like this with all the people you work with?" she asked.

"I care about all my clients because they are people. People really aren't so bad. As for Kyle, I've become closer to him than to a lot of my clients. Part of that was Daisy. Part of it Kyle."

Lincoln finished off his glass of wine and leaned in closer to her. Maddie's eyes widened and her cheeks felt warm. The only way she could describe how she felt was flustered, and she did not like it. Taking the last drink of her wine, she quickly stood up and felt herself sway.

Standing up, Lincoln grabbed her arm and laughed. "I forgot to warn you about the wine. It packs a punch."

Maddie stammered, "I guess it does. We should go to bed." Realizing what she said, she gasped. "Me! I meant I should go to bed."

Before she could walk away, Lincoln pulled her closer. "You know, sometimes you just have to let go. You keep yourself so…I don't know…controlled."

Maddie stared at him, at his lips and wished things were different. As Lincoln leaned in closer, she pulled away and hurried to the kitchen where she left her glass on the counter. No sense in getting involved with anyone right now, especially Lincoln. It would only complicate things even more than they already were.

***

Maddie sat in the office looking over the information she had uploaded onto the computer. As it was, she had a website for Dandelion Farm, but not one product.

Well, she had the products her aunt had made and sitting in the cupboards, but if she were going to do this, she had to figure out how to make the products herself. It was a good thing the website was not live yet. Before she hit the button, she would have to see exactly what she was capable of in the kitchen.

Standing up, she laughed as Peaches stood, stretched, and yawned. Over the last week, the dog was eating normally and following her around wherever she went, except outside. Peaches was an inside dog and wanted nothing to do with the farm animals. The new puppy, Dudley, liked to annoy her, but Peaches had put him in his place many times.

In the kitchen, Maddie set the recipe for dandelion jelly on the counter and gathered the supplies. Once everything was prepped, she grabbed a large bowl and headed outside. Dandelions filled the fields. As a little girl, she had run through this field and enjoyed many picnics with her aunt. Perhaps Kyle had done the same?

Thoughts of Kyle led her to thoughts of Lincoln. Ever since Wednesday evening when he had tried to kiss her, she had been avoiding him. *Avoid was probably a strong word,* she thought, but either way, she hadn't exactly had much one-on-one time with him. The one night they did, he casually asked her if she wanted to go out to dinner some night with him. He offered to have someone come stay with Kyle, but she politely declined. Too much to do around this place was her excuse.

Maddie checked each dandelion over to make certain it was prime for picking. According to her aunt's notes, she wanted the ones that appeared to have recently opened. No brown marks and none looking sad. Maddie had questioned the last statement until now. It was quite easy to see the difference between the ones she would use for jelly and the ones not worth picking.

A shadow loomed over her and Maddie jumped back several steps fearing one of the cows had decided to intrude on her. Seeing Lincoln, she groaned.

"Do you get a kick out of startling me?" she snapped.

Lincoln grinned. "Not at all. I figured you would have heard me coming."

"I didn't."

"I see that. Need some help?"

The bowl not even half-full, Maddie looked around. How long would it take one person to pick a bowl full of dandelions? Judging by how long it had taken already—a long time— Maddie reluctantly nodded her head.

Lincoln was silent and leaned over and started picking the ones in front of him. "No, no! You have to be selective. Only pick the ones that look like they just opened. Those have brown on the edges. You also got to watch for bugs. None with bugs."

"Well, you could make speckled jelly," Lincoln joked.

"I'll make that special for you another time, but right now, I want to see if I can make her jelly and have it taste like hers."

"That's good. I ran into Henry Springer the other day. He asked about the jelly and placed an order for a dozen half-pints. I forgot to tell you."

Maddie's jaw dropped. "You took an order? I haven't even made this before. And then you forgot to tell me? Lincoln…"

"Don't go getting all frustrated, Maddie. Henry has a small store at the edge of town, and he likes to keep it in stock. No biggie if he has to wait a bit."

Maddie snapped. "It is a big deal to me. I'm the one that has to try to make something I hope will live up to my aunt's product. What if I blow it? What if I can't do it? And you've already promised him some?"

What was he thinking? Maddie leaned over and ripped dandelions out of the ground, throwing them into the bowl. *He's just here taking a break from work. This is my life,* she thought. *Mine! Not his. Yet, he kind of acts like he's the boss around here. Well, he might be Kyle's boss, but he's not mine.* "Not by a long shot," she muttered to herself.

When she looked up, Lincoln was striding back across the field toward the farmhouse. Shoulders slumped, she let out a sigh. It was not as if she wanted to be mad at him, but first the puppy and now this. Today was supposed to be a relaxing day of trying to can some jelly. Now she had Lincoln mad at her. He could have at least apologized to her. But no! He let her go off the deep end and then walked away. Who does that? *Not me,* she thought, and she then wondered if that were a good thing or a bad thing.

In the kitchen, Maddie surveyed the mess and checked the time again. Two minutes left before she could shut the heat off. The canning process was not difficult, but everything had to be precise. Not paying attention to the time could be cause for the jelly not to set, so her eyes barely left the clock. Ten minutes had never seemed so long.

As soon as the timer sounded, Maddie quickly turned off the heat and removed the large pot from the stove and placed it on the wooden cutting board. After removing the lid, she set the timer again for five-minutes and started to clean the mess. She was not exactly a great cook, but she always liked to clean as she cooked. The timer went off as soon as the kitchen was cleaned up and she smiled. Time to see if they looked good. Using the jar grabber, she lifted the first half-pint jar to find the lid scrunched up and bent. Setting it down on the dish towel, she moved on to the next relieved to find this one looked better. After removing the other ten jars, she let out the breath she had been holding. Eleven out of twelve jars looked good, but that was just the first part. Once they cooled down, she and Kyle would be able to taste them. That would be the real test.

Looking at the jar with the messed-up lid, she wondered if she could use that one for the taste test. Was it even safe? Running into the office with Peaches on her heels, she grabbed the book on canning she had been studying. After finding the information she needed, she smiled. With a buckled lid, she could not store it, but it would be perfect for the taste test.

Kyle was at work for another hour. Lincoln would be picking him up. She had not seen him since yesterday when she had gone off on him, and the thought made her cringe. She hadn't meant to. She hated when anyone pushed her. Perhaps it was the Taurus in her coming out? Laughing, she realized Kyra must be on her mind. Kyra was the one who followed astrology—not her. When she saw Lincoln again, *if* she saw Lincoln again, she would apologize.

Realizing she was as impatient as a person could be, she grabbed a spoon and opened the warm jar. The color reminded her of honey. All that work cleaning the dandelions paid off. The worst part of the process had been letting the dandelions soak in water over night. Making this jelly certainly was not quick, which made her chuckle. She was always a person who liked instant gratification. She liked to see results quickly and even Wendy would tell her to slow down when she wanted to revamp an ad campaign if the results did not happen soon enough.

That, of course, made her wonder if farm-life would be enough for her. While she was not an adrenaline junkie, she liked to be busy. Standing around waiting for something to happen was not exactly her style. Looking down at the work boots on her feet, she shrugged. Those were not exactly her style either, but she seemed to have gotten used to them.

Dipping the spoon into the jar of jelly, she brought it to her lips. Sticky and sweet, she could only compare it to honey. When she had read about making dandelion jelly, she had learned they called it 'poor man's honey', and she could see why. It was remarkably similar. She just hoped it would compare to her aunt's. The last thing she wanted was to be the killer of her aunt's dreams.

Chapter Twelve

Maddie peeked out the window again. She had not talked to Lincoln in over a week. It had gone from being a silly little argument to one drawn out, and one leaving her feeling almost ill. Kyle, thankfully, had not commented that Lincoln was not coming in the house. Basically, Lincoln showed up, helped Kyle with the chores, and left. While he still took Kyle back and forth to work, he had not spoken a word to her. She was not sure if he was overreacting or she was. Seeing him coming around the corner of the barn toward the house, Maddie ducked.

Staying low, she crept into the living room. If Lincoln was coming in the house to see her, she did not want him to find her peeking out the window. In the office she quickly turned on the computer and let out her breath. The sound of an engine started, and she knew Lincoln was leaving. He had not wanted to see her after all. Peaches whined at her feet, and Maddie reached down to pick her up. "I'm glad someone loves me. And I love you, Miss Peaches." Snuggling the little dog to her chest, she leaned back in the chair. She did not need Lincoln to love her, but it would be nice if he cared enough to check in on her. An apology would be nice, too.

The office was looking much better and over the last week, she and Kyle had formed somewhat of a routine. It was not perfect, but it worked for them. While Lincoln had been helping with morning chores before taking Kyle to work, and occasionally helped in the late afternoon, she and Kyle did the evening chores together. She was quite good at shoveling manure, feeding the animals, and even corralling them into the barn at night. The hardest part of the whole thing was figuring out what to do with the business.

After getting a dozen jars of dandelion jelly ready for Henry, she was quick to find out from his wife, Helen, she was unable to sell any food products until she received a license to do so. The current license was under her aunt's name and, until she had everything changed to her own name, she was unable to sell a thing. The upside of that—it would give her more time for planning and, perhaps, creating a few new products to add to the line.

Her aunt had some great recipes to try. Some of them might even interest Kyra. A facial mask made from goat's milk and oats. She used the one in the bathroom and could not believe the difference it made. While she had always taken good care of her skin, this formula was much better than any of the expensive products she used. It only took a few days for her to see a difference. Her skin was softer and looked fabulous. Perhaps mailing a sample to Kyra would give her a better idea of whether it would sell.

The state license had already been filled out and sent in, but she was not sure if the change would require another inspection. She had read the rules. The hardest part would be keeping Peaches out of the kitchen when she was making products. While the other dogs claimed the living room and sometimes spent the day outside, except Mutley, of course, Peaches was underfoot all the time. Locking her in the office seemed to be the only way she could get anything done.

A door banging brought Maddie back from her thoughts and she listened as footsteps came closer. In seconds, Lincoln made an appearance in the doorway. "Can you come with me? I want to show you something."

Maddie got up from the desk and tripped over the pile of magazines on the floor. It was the first time he had spoken to her in about a week, and he did not even ask her how she was doing. His long legs caused for long strides, and Maddie did her best to keep close behind him.

"What's going on?" she asked.

Lincoln did not say anything. When they reached the barn, he stopped and turned around to her. "Did you know about this?" His arm stretched out to point out the small donkey in the front stall. Only about forty-eight inches tall, it was thin, and a lot of fur was missing from its back. The donkey brayed and stomped its front feet.

Maddie looked up at Lincoln, her eyes wide. "No, I didn't. Kyle?"

The donkey brayed louder and pushed against the gate. Maddie took a step forward and tried to soothe the donkey. "It's alright, sweetheart. Nobody's going to hurt you."

"Kyle's been at work all morning. Was it here this morning?" Lincoln reached over and petted the top of the donkey's head. In response, the donkey tried to bite him.

"Oh, guess it's not that fond of people. No. It wasn't here when Kyle and I let the other animals out. I've been home all morning, but I've pretty much been cooped up in the office."

"Well, Daisy used to take in strays all the time and people would always drop them off without a word. I'd say either someone doesn't know Daisy is gone, or they just figured you would take the donkey in like she would."

"Lincoln, how can we keep another donkey? Marvin and Madelyn are good donkeys, but this one? What do I do?" Maddie reached out to pet the donkey, and like it did to Lincoln, it tried to bite her. "It obviously hates people."

Lincoln crossed his arms over his chest. "You sure you want me to say anything? I don't want to interfere in how you manage your farm?"

Maddie groaned. So, that was how it was going to be. "Lincoln, I really didn't mean to snap at you or hurt your feelings about the jelly, but…"

"You didn't hurt my feelings. I figured you needed some space."

"Space? You ignore me for over a week and that's your excuse?" Maddie watched for any signs Lincoln was messing around with her and could see none. He was absolutely serious. Exasperated, she asked, "Is that how you handle your clients?"

Lincoln massaged his temples. "Maddie, I am just saying I thought you needed space. If you didn't need space, you could have come out to talk to me. Regardless, right now, you need to figure out what you are going to do with this donkey."

Maddie did not know. The donkey appeared to be fine, as long as no one reached out to touch it. Looking down, she said, "It's a he. First things first, I'll call the vet to come check him out. He will also need a name. I say we let him stay in the stall until the vet clears him. Then we can introduce him to the others."

Lincoln nodded his head. "I'll get some food and water for him, throw a little more hay in, and see what happens. Maybe he'll calm down once he's had some food."

"Are you saying he's hangry?" she joked.

Lincoln groaned. "Seriously?"

Maddie laughed. "Well, at least we're laughing."

"You have a point. So, what are you going to name this guy?"

"I'm not sure. Maybe Hank? Then we can call him Cranky Hanky," Maddie suggested.

"That has got to be the worst thing I've ever heard come out of your mouth." Lincoln laughed. "Cranky Hanky?"

Maddie moved to stand in front of the stall where the donkey stood. The donkey brayed and stomped his feet.

"Well, it's not like we could call him Cuddles. I think Hank is a good name."

"Hank it is," Lincoln said. Grabbing a piece of chalk, he wrote the name Hank on the chalkboard beside the stall. "Let's hope nobody else drops off anymore animals or you're going to run out of space."

Concern covered Maddie's face. "What would Aunt Daisy do?"

Laughing, Lincoln threw his hands in the air. "Your aunt would build a bigger barn. But this is your place now. Only you can make that decision."

Maddie shook her head. "No. It's not just mine. This place is Kyle's home. But I already know what he'll say."

"But you need to remember something important. Kyle is not the boss. The minute you let him believe he is the boss, he is going to take charge on a level you are not ready for. And you shouldn't be. You need to remember Kyle is not looking at things from your level of wisdom and experience. Kyle is looking at things from the perspective of an eight to ten-year-old."

Nodding her head, Maddie added. "I didn't mean he was the boss. I meant he's been through so many changes already. I don't want to take his way-of-life away from him because it inconveniences me."

"Kyle's a good kid. He bounces back quite well. If he has someone to love him, food on the table, and a few pets around, he's happy."

At the mention of food, Maddie's stomach grumbled. "I'm making quesadillas for dinner. Do you want to stay?"

"Sure. Anything you need me to get when I pick up Kyle?"

"Nope, already got everything I need," Maddie said and turned to go back to the house, confused as to how they went from not speaking for a week to Lincoln staying for supper.

***

Charging through the door, Kyle yelled, "Maddie! Lincoln's staying for supper."

Standing at the sink doing dishes, Maddie smiled. Kyle's excitement matched her own, but she did not let it show. It had been over a week since Lincoln sat down for dinner at the table with them. While she knew in her head she and Lincoln could not—or rather should not—be more

124

than friends, Kyle enjoyed having him around. So did she. *But only as a friend*, she said to herself.

Kyle raced upstairs to get washed up as Lincoln walked through the door. It seemed strange to have him in the kitchen again. It was almost as strange as what it felt like when he stopped sleeping in the room down the hall. Maddie grabbed the dish towel and wiped her hands. "Do you want to wash up here?"

Striding across the floor, Lincoln stood in front of the sink, inches away from her. Feeling her face turning hot, Maddie backed off and moved in front of the stove where she was heating up some refried beans. Along with a corn salad she already made, she was serving some guacamole and pickled jalapenos she found in the cupboard. Not sure exactly how much Kyle liked spicy Mexican food, she had also made some nachos.

"I don't know what you're doing, but something smells fantastic in here," Lincoln stated as he wiped his hands dry. Leaning over toward Maddie, he grabbed a spoon, dipped it into the guacamole and tasted it. "Oh, that's good. I'm starving now."

Kyle stomped down the stairs with both Mutley and Dudley following close behind him. "I'm hungry, Maddie."

Laughing, Maddie replied, "You two go sit down. I'll get stuff ready to bring to the table."

Kyle and Lincoln seated themselves at the table, and Maddie got to work. The quesadillas were done and warming in the oven. Everything else was ready to go and she brought the dishes to the table. Kyle's mouth hung open when he saw the dishes arrive. "What is this?"

"It's Mexican food. Have you ever had it before?" Lincoln asked.

"No. I don't know. Mum wasn't Mexican." He picked up a piece of his quesadilla and took a big bite. "Yum!" With more enthusiasm, he took another big bite, causing Lincoln and Maddie to laugh.

"Well, I am glad you like them. Mexican dishes are some of my favorite to make." Maddie filled her plate, feeling the happiest she had felt all week. Most nights, she and Kyle ate dinner in almost silence, neither seeming too comfortable yet with their company. Tonight, Kyle was more vocal and, obviously, happy to have Lincoln at table with them.

She could not really blame Kyle, though. She had been so busy trying to figure out licensing for the farm and new products to try out she had not been too attentive herself. Between the business end of things and all the chores that had to be done daily, there was not a lot of time left for fun. This was something she needed to change.

"You guys up for a movie tonight? Or maybe a game of *Monopoly*?" Maddie asked.

"Movie!" Kyle replied. "Let's watch *Homeward Bound*!"

"Kyle, haven't you already watched that movie about a hundred times?" Lincoln winked at Maddie.

"Yes, but it's my favorite. Shadow is my favorite, but I would keep Chance and Sassy, too. They run away from their babysitter and get lost. But then they come home. Mum always cried at that part. Not me."

Maddie leaned over and whispered to Kyle, "It's one of my favorites, too. I say let's watch it."

A grin came over Kyle's face as he reached out for some nachos, and she turned to look at Lincoln who was also smiling. "You in?"

"Of course I am. It's a great movie!"

***

When the movie ended, Lincoln stood up. "Well, I'm going to take off. Anything you need before I leave?"

Kyle stood up, too. "I'm going to take the dogs out and go to bed. I got tomorrow off, Lincoln. Don't forget."

"I won't. Do you guys have any plans? I was thinking maybe we could take Maddie around town. Maybe we can ask around about the donkey? See if anyone knows anything."

Kyle called all the dogs outside, leaving Lincoln and Maddie alone.

"I guess so. Maybe we can take Kyle to lunch somewhere? I've been here two weeks and haven't really gone anywhere but the market."

"Sounds like a plan. After morning chores are done, we can head out."

As Lincoln walked into the kitchen, he turned back around toward Maddie who was still seated on the couch. "Thanks for dinner again. It was amazing."

"You're welcome. I don't cook much, but Mexican food is pretty easy."

"It was great. I'll see you in the morning."

Maddie watched as he let himself out the door as Kyle was coming inside with the dogs trailing behind him. Jack went to his corner in the dining room and both Bella and Lily claimed their spots on the couch beside her. Peaches jumped up in her lap, and both Mutley and Dudley followed Kyle up the stairs. That was the one thing she was having trouble getting used to.

In Boston, her normal routine was going to bed at midnight after finishing up the work she brought home and getting up at six to do it all over again. Now, she was exhausted by eight after doing chores. One thing could be said for farm work, though. She no longer needed a gym. The work around the farm had tightened muscles and her arms were already showing a difference. Her pants were fitting her a little more loosely as well, which did not make sense because she had never been hungrier. All this work was good for her body.

Wandering around the downstairs, Maddie said goodnight to all the dogs and shut off the lights. The moonlight shined through the windows, and Maddie peered outside. Peaceful was the only word she could come up with to describe it. The animals were all tucked into the barn for the night, all the chores were done, and Kyle had gone to bed happy.

Wandering back into the living room, Maddie looked around. She should go to bed but knew she would never sleep. Maybe it was having Lincoln around tonight. Who knew? Instead of going upstairs to her own room, she entered her aunt's room and turned on the light.

Her aunt's journal still sat on the desk. Picking it up, she read from the beginning, which was almost two years ago.

"Oh, if you could have seen him. The pig didn't even hesitate to plow that boy right over. There he sat in the middle of the pig pen, covered in mud and God knows what else. The biggest grin came across that boy's face. Kyle was

hysterical with laughter. We needed that. While Lincoln may not know much about pigs, he certainly has a great attitude. He's going to be great for Kyle."

Maddie could picture that happening. Daisy was on the mark when it came to Lincoln. He was great for Kyle. Kyle had been sullen the whole week when Lincoln was not staying there or eating dinner with him. Tonight, Kyle had been animated and full of life. With only her for company, it was not the same. Did Daisy make the right choice? She obviously was not the right choice if Kyle was not happy. Regretting her decision to read the journal, Maddie placed it back on the desk. Feeling like a deflated balloon, she went to her room and let the tears flow. She had given up everything—her whole life—to come here. What if it was not enough for Kyle? Or her?

Chapter Thirteen

Pressing the label onto the jar of dandelion jelly, Maddie looked at the counter with pride. Her jelly tasted exactly like her aunt's. But that was only due to her aunt's diligence in creating a recipe that was unique and descriptive. While her aunt had never created a label for her products, it was one of Maddie's first steps to expand the business. In the last two weeks, she had done a lot. The license was now hanging in the kitchen in the exact same spot her aunt had hung hers. The label she created had a picture of dandelions on it with the name Dandelion Farms above it. The name of the product was underneath with the ingredients listed below. Holding the jar up to the light, Maddie squealed with delight. She was not normally so vocal, but the whole project was hers from start to finish.

She had worked in marketing and helped create some of the best advertisements for some great products, yet she never had complete creative control. Now, in her aunt's business—her business—she could take chances, take risks, and make all the decisions. Whether she succeeded or failed, she would take something from it.

Even though her products were based around dandelions, she had tried a few other recipes her aunt had. The violet jelly was sure to be a big hit. The only way she could describe the flavor was summer. It tasted like summer. The jelly ended up a beautiful, light purple, and she had simply changed the color on the font on the labels to purple. It looked fantastic. It was easy enough to do and made a huge difference in differentiating the products.

Kyle had loved the idea, too, but his favorite way to help was trying out the different things she was making. Dandelion ice cream was his favorite so far. While she knew it would be a hit, the problem she was having was with packaging. She had yet to figure out a way to do it as cheaply as she would like. To keep her products at a reasonable price and still make a profit, she had to figure out a way to keep the costs down.

Two weeks ago, she wanted to quit after reading in her aunt's journal how great Lincoln was with Kyle. Seeing the difference in Kyle when Lincoln was around put her into a funk that lasted a few days. Then one day she and Kyle cleaned out the barn and played with the donkeys. He laughed and played, and Maddie realized in that moment exactly how much she had grown to care about him. Leave him? No way.

She had also grown closer to Lincoln. No, he was no longer staying at the farm but every evening, they would have dinner together, do chores together, and if Kyle was in the mood, they played a game or watched a movie. Lincoln was also a great taste-tester. He had tried almost everything her Aunt Daisy made, so he was the perfect guinea pig. The first time he tried her dandelion tea, he had wrinkled up his nose. "Nope, somethings missing," he told her. It only took her a few minutes to discover she had left out the lemon juice by accident.

Now that she had the license, had come up with a business logo, and had products to sell, it was a matter of getting them to the public. First, she would deliver to Henry, who had already placed an order with Lincoln. That made her cringe as it reminded her of how she had flipped out and caused Lincoln to stay away for a week. As she packed up jellies into boxes, she made a vow she would not snap again.

Swinging into the parking lot of *H. G. Gardiner's Mini-Mart*, Maddie took a deep breath. She knew Henry had wanted a dozen jars of the dandelion jelly, but she had come with a plan. Along with the dandelion jelly, she had brought a dozen of the violet jelly and some blueberry jam. She also had brought a few jars of the goat's milk and oatmeal facial mask she made. As it was made from all-natural ingredients, it should interest some people.

Stepping into the store with her boxes of products in her arms, she smiled at the gentleman at the counter. "Are you Henry?"

"Well, young lady, you are correct in your assumption. Set those boxes right here, Miss Madelyn from Boston."

"You know who I am?" She set the boxes down on the counter and took a step back.

"Of course I do. I was at your aunt's service. Me and Daisy went way back. Before I married Helen, I tried to date her, but she weren't having none of that." He chuckled. "I weren't the only one she turned down, though. Miss Daisy was a fine woman. She's missed around here."

"I am so sorry I don't remember meeting you. It was such a hard day."

"No worries. I take it you've got some of her dandelion jelly?"

"I do. I followed her recipes exactly. I'm going to keep her business going for her and Kyle."

"Your aunt would be proud of you." He opened the box with the facial masks and raised his right eyebrow. "This don't look like jelly to me."

"No, it's not. The dandelion jelly is in the other box. This is something special I made from another one of my aunt's recipes. It is a facial mask for women. It's made from goat's milk and oatmeal. Only natural ingredients, so it does not contain any toxins at all. Women will find it refreshing, and it makes their skin feel softer. I was wondering if you'd want to keep a couple here and see if they sell."

With a twinkle in his eye, Henry asked, "Think it will do this old kisser any good?"

Maddie giggled. She had already fallen in love with the man. "You look perfect just the way you are."

"Now I know you'll say anything to get your stuff on my shelves! But, yes, we can try. What else you got?"

"I also made some of her violet jelly and some blueberry jam. I'm not sure what you had set up with Daisy, but what do you sell them for? Is it a split of the profit?"

"I sell them for $8.99 a jar. I get a third of it and you get the rest. How does that sound?"

"Perfect. The facial mask and any lotions, though, will be a higher price. How about you try selling them for $14.99?" Maddie replied.

"This is perfect, young lady. We get regulars in here all the time that are always asking for Daisy's stuff. They'll be happy with more options. Poor Daisy did her best, but she always had so much on her plate with Kyle and all those animals. You still got her animals?”

“I do and, yes, it’s a lot of work, but Kyle’s already been through too much to make any more changes.”

Henry rubbed his chin. “You’ll be good for that boy. Daisy did a great job and I’m sure you will, too.”

“Thank you so much. I appreciate that. Any idea where else I can place some of this product?”

“I always tried to convince Daisy to do the Farmer’s Market on Saturdays. She always said, ‘Now Henry, you know Saturdays are the busiest.’ You would be surprised by how many people are there on Saturday mornings. It might be a good place to start.”

“Oh, yes. I didn’t even know there was a Farmer’s Market. Do you know who I have to contact?”

“Just give Jimmy Brown a call. He and his wife started it. They’ll tell you what to do.”

Excitement ran through Maddie’s veins during her drive home. The Farmer’s Market could be what she needed to get more product sold. She had all the books set up and could not wait to start listing some sales in them. Sadly, Daisy had not really kept good track of her profits, but she was determined to make this work and get the farm in the black.

***

“Are you ready, Maddie?” Kyle was as excited to go to the Farmer’s Market as she was. But a smooth morning it was not. Hank, who had made himself at home after getting cleared by the vet, was trying to be Houdini. He was a little underweight, but he was certainly making up for lost time. This morning she had found him in the middle of the

134

garden eating the green beans that had started producing a few weeks before. His attitude still was not great, but she had managed to get him back in the pen with the others and repaired the fence where he had pushed through.

"Kyle, I just need to grab some sunscreen and put the cooler in the car. We'll be out in the sun all morning."

"I'll put the cooler in the car. Come on. Everyone's going to be there already."

Laughing, Maddie hurried along. While Kyle said he had been to the Farmer's Market, he had never gone as a seller. Today, Kyle was going to be helping her to sell, and his excitement only made her own grow. This could be what was needed for them both. Until now, she was pretty much doing things on her own. She would run things by Kyle, but he had never been as enthusiastic about anything like this. After arriving at the Farmer's Market, which was located right on Main Street in the park, Maddie and Kyle unloaded the car, set up the table and umbrella, and carefully arranged their products on the dandelion tablecloth she had found in the cupboard. It was perfect. Telling Kyle to stand behind the table, Maddie took out her camera and snapped a picture of him with a wide grin on his face. It would be the perfect photo for their website.

"Why don't you get in there and let me get a picture of the two of you together?"

Maddie gasped. "Lincoln, you came."

"Kyle's been talking about this all week long."

Maddie's shoulders slumped. Of course. Kyle was Lincoln's concern, and Lincoln always took care of his clients. "Yes. That would be great." Moving behind the table beside Kyle, she wrapped her arm around him and smiled for the camera.

"This is awesome," Lincoln said and showed Maddie and Kyle the picture he took.

"Okay, let's sell some stuff," Kyle stated.

And sell they did. About an hour before the end of the day they sold out, and Maddie had taken several orders. The biggest hit surprised her. Women of all ages requested her facial mask. The dozen jars she brought were gone in the first hour. By the end of the day, she had orders for another two dozen. How she would have time to fill them all, she had no idea. Feeling a little overwhelmed when they got home, she watched Kyle count their earnings for the day and knew she had made the right decision to include him.

"Maddie, we made six-hundred dollars! We're rich!" he yelled.

"Not rich, Kyle, but we're doing okay." Kyle did not have a clue to the fortune his mother had left for him. "Your mother was a very smart woman, Kyle. She made sure you have enough money."

"Then why do I have a job?" he asked.

"Do you like working at your job?"

"Yes. I love my job." Kyle grinned. "That's why I have my job."

"You are correct. When you love something the way you love your job, you can't give it up."

"Did you love your job, Maddie? The one you had before you came here to live?"

Maddie shook her head. "No, I thought I did. But once I came here, I realized just how much I didn't like it."

"I'm glad you came, Maddie!" Kyle gave her one of the sweetest smiles she had seen on his face. Maddie realized in that moment that she, too, was happy she came to Cove's Port.

***

Opening the freezer door, Maddie gagged. Slamming it shut, Maddie ran to the door and opened it. Fresh air filled her lungs. Leaning over the rail, Maddie sucked it in quickly, hoping the gag reflex would stop. Kyle was at work and Lincoln was at a meeting. Just her luck she would find something like that without anyone there to help her.

Running into the house, she grabbed one of her shirts off the chair and wrapped it around her face. Anything to keep the smell away. In front of the freezer, she took a deep breath and then carefully opened it. Everything, meat, milk, vegetables, and bread, was thawed out and rotting. Shutting the door again, Maddie ran to the other freezer. Thankfully, this one was still operating, and she leaned against it.

Over half of the goat's milk had been in the freezer. Going back over to it, she leaned down and checked the back. The power cord was unplugged and tucked behind the freezer. Someone had unplugged it. Gasping, Maddie picked the power cord up and threw it back down. Kicking the freezer, she groaned. A throbbing foot was not what she needed either.

Grabbing some garbage bags and bleach, Maddie set out to work. She was not sure if the freezer could even be saved. Two hours later, as Lincoln drove into the driveway with Kyle beside him in the truck, Maddie frowned. Her

137

whole afternoon had been wasted on this mess. The kitchen was a mess, too, as she had planned on working on some of the orders today.

"What's going on?" Lincoln asked as he saw the garbage bags lining the walkway. Plugging his nose, he asked, "What is that?"

Maddie wiped the sweat from her brow. "That is everything that was in one of the freezers."

Kyle came running up to stand beside Lincoln. "Oh, Maddie! That's gross." Plugging his nose, he ran past her and into the house.

"What happened?" Lincoln walked by the bags and up onto the porch where Maddie was standing.

Maddie groaned. "Someone must have unplugged the freezer. Everything inside it was rotten. Not sure how long ago it happened. I haven't been in the freezer for almost two weeks."

Lincoln's mouth dropped open. "Oh my God, Maddie! I unplugged it last week when I needed to plug in the drill to fix the doorstep. I must have forgotten to plug it back in."

Maddie swore inside her head. At least she hoped those words stayed inside. Taking a breath, she looked at him calmly, or at least hoping she looked calm. Inside she was seething. "You forgot?"

Lincoln stepped forward and grabbed her arm. "I am so sorry. I can't believe I did that. What's left to be done?"

Maddie did not know what to say. The vegetables and bread? No big deal. All the meat that was lost would be replaced when she slaughtered the pigs in a few weeks. But the goat's milk? That would take a while to get back if she could. Right now, she had more orders than what the milking goat produced in a week. All she could do was be on top of the milking and hope for the best.

"I have it all cleaned out already. I was going to throw some baking soda in it and see if it would help with the smell."

Lincoln stepped off the porch. "Okay. I'm going to load these up in my truck to take over to the dump. Maddie, I am so sorry. Why don't I stop and get us a pizza for dinner? It looks like you've done enough work for today. You shouldn't have to worry about cooking tonight."

Maddie grunted. "Sure. I'll see you when you get back."

Going over to the other freezer, Maddie opened the door. Five gallons of goat's milk. So, it was not as bad as what she thought. Ten gallons were thrown away. She still had five along with the typical half-gallon a day she got from Betty. All was not lost, but the disaster had woken her up. She had to watch everything that was done around the farm to make sure it was done right.

Chapter Fourteen

Exhaustion hit Maddie like a ton of bricks. Over the last several days, she had made five dozen jars of the facial mask, five dozen of a goat's milk lotion, and several dozen jars of jelly. She would be alone at the Farmer's Market today as Kyle was on the schedule to work. It was exciting, but Maddie wished she could stay in bed longer. She may not have missed her life in Boston, but she sure missed the weekends when she could sleep in. This six o'clock in the morning thing was getting old.

Downstairs, she turned the coffee pot on, threw on a jacket as it was chilly in the mornings, and walked out to the barn to milk the goat. She contemplated getting another milking goat but did not want to overdo it too soon. If things went as well as she expected them to, she could always buy goat milk from some of the local dairies.

Once the morning chores were done, and she put the goat's milk in the refrigerator, Maddie started getting breakfast ready for Kyle. The routine of the morning was enjoyable. She had even gotten used to her attire. The jeans she had brought with her had now been replaced by more sturdy ones. Her Jimmy *Choos* were packed away in the closet and, while she still loved all her shoes, she really did not miss how they made her feet feel. The work boots she had bought at *Ray's Market* were now well-worn and she rarely went without wearing them.

Kyle came down the stairs and took the dogs out without a word to her. When he came back in, Kyle stood in front of her. "Maddie, I want to go to the Farmer's Market with you."

"Oh, Buddy, I wish you could to. Maybe we can talk to Ray about you taking off Saturdays until the Farmer's Market closes for the year. That way, you can be there every Saturday from now on."

Kyle nodded, but stood in place. "But I want to go today."

"I know you do, but Ray is expecting you at work. You don't want to leave him without any help."

Groaning, Kyle sat down at the table where Maddie had put his plate. "You can't go, Kyle. You can't go," he grumbled.

Turning back to the stove, Maddie grinned. When she first arrived, Kyle's self-talk had made her uneasy. Now, it was the norm. She even found she talked to herself more often than she ever did. Kyle had taught her one thing—it was okay to use words to calm yourself down. She had done that many times over the last week.

She had held herself back from going nuts over the freezer catastrophe. But it was getting tougher to keep an eye on Lincoln all week. One day, he left the gate open to the pigs. She had rushed in to shut it just in time and realized the last time they got out Lincoln had been the last one to take care of them. Another day, he left the water running to the trough in the donkey pen. Mumbling and grumbling, she simply turned the water off and watched for the next mistake. No wonder she was tired.

***

The Farmer's Market was already busy when she arrived, and she set up as quickly as possible as a line had already started to form in front of her booth. A half-hour later and Maddie had the line cleared when she saw Mrs. Drummond walking her way.

"Mrs. Drummond, how are you?"

"Oh, Madelyn. Daisy would love this. She always wanted to do this, but claimed she never had the time." Mrs. Drummond leaned over to inspect the different products on the table.

"Thank you. It is hard to find the time, but I want to do right by her." Maddie reached up and swept her hair into a ponytail. She had found her hair was another thing she could not keep up with. Going to the salon to have highlights and a fresh cut every six weeks was not going to happen around here.

"You've done great. What do you have here? Is this the facial stuff I've heard so much about? Emma and Phyllis told me all about it. I have to say I believe them after seeing their wrinkly, old faces looking better than they have in years."

Maddie almost laughed but saw the seriousness on Mrs. Drummond's face. "I have some of the facial mask right here, but I also made goat's milk lotion if you would rather have that," she said and picked up the small container to show her.

"I'll take them both," she said and then leaned in closer. "I heard you took in a puppy a while back. Any chance you got any more? Our little pug, Jackie, died a few months ago, and I think we're ready for another dog."

"I'm so sorry. We did take in a puppy, but I believe Kyle has become quite attached. I will talk to him, though. Dudley is a small terrier-mix that would be perfect for you."

"Oh, good. Let Kyle know I would take good care of him. But I won't get my hopes up. I know how Kyle is with animals," Mrs. Drummond said. "Daisy let him keep whatever he wanted."

"I promise I'll speak to him," Maddie said as she took the cash and put it in the cashbox. "I will let you know."

After Mrs. Drummond left, it seemed like there were no breaks. Again, she was sold out before the end of the day. Every penny earned from the market was going right back into the business. If she were going to continue this, though, she would have to find a bigger vehicle. She had her *Camry* and Daisy's old car sat in the driveway, but neither afforded her a lot of room. A minivan would probably be the best thing, which caused her to wince. A minivan? Never in her life did she think she would ever consider buying one.

As she was packing up for the day, Lincoln stopped in and offered to help.

"I take it by the looks of your empty boxes that today was another success?" he asked.

Maddie grinned. "I can't believe how well things are selling. Even my new lotion sold out."

"That's great. I know Kyle was upset he couldn't help you out today. I'll talk to Ray about changing his schedule so he can be here every Saturday if you want."

"That would be great. I felt so bad this morning. Oh! Mrs. Drummond stopped by today. She is looking for a new puppy and I thought I would talk to Kyle about Dudley."

Lincoln's squinted his eyes and set the box down. "Maddie that's not a good idea."

"I didn't say I was going to take the puppy away. I thought I would ask if he thought Dudley would be a good dog for Mrs. Drummond—see what he thinks."

"No. You can't do that. Kyle will not even consider it. Why get him upset?"

Groaning, Maddie clasped her hands together. Why was it that every time she made a suggestion about Kyle, Lincoln would shoot her down? Last week, she had suggested Kyle get involved with the local softball team and Lincoln came out and said no. He did not even explain why he did not think it was a good idea.

Grabbing a couple of empty boxes, Maddie stated, "Well, I think it's a good idea. Even if he says no, it will get through to him that the next puppy that comes along must go to another home. We can't keep anymore."

Lincoln picked up some boxes and followed behind her to her car. "I get what you're saying, Maddie. No, you don't need any more dogs, but you cannot take Dudley away when he's already become so attached."

Turning around to face him, Maddie's voice rose, "I know he's attached. But he is only attached because you told him he could keep the puppy without even asking me. Remember?"

"How could I forget when you keep reminding me?" he snapped. Within seconds, he was apologizing. "I get it,

Maddie. I messed up, and I am sorry. But you can't try to take Dudley away."

Maddie slammed the trunk. "I am not trying to take Dudley away. How many times do I have to tell you that?"

Lincoln stepped back and watched Maddie grab the rest of her stuff. "You want me to pick up Kyle from work for you today?"

"No, I'll get him. As a matter of fact, I have taken you away from your job enough. From now on, I'll take Kyle to work and pick him up every day, so you don't have to. I don't want to take advantage anymore."

Lincoln nodded. "Okay. I guess that's that."

As Lincoln walked away, Maddie leaned against her car. She had been planning on telling Lincoln he did not need to transport Kyle back and forth to work anymore but not in that way. Now he thought she was doing it out of spite. *One more thing I messed up*, she thought and got in the car to go get Kyle from work.

***

"No, Maddie! She can't have my dog," Kyle yelled.

"Kyle, it's okay. I told her I would ask you. That's all," Maddie soothed. Or at least she tried. Inside, she was frantic and wanted to slap Lincoln for being right. Why did he have to be right all the time?

"You can't take Dudley. He's Mutley's best friend." Kyle stood in front of her, hands on his hips and his jaw straight out. His voice was low, and his eyes narrowed. Maddie knew she was in trouble.

"Kyle, Dudley's not going anywhere. Okay?" She reached out to touch his arm, and Kyle stepped back.

145

"My dog is my dog. You can't ever take my dogs away."

"I know, Kyle."

"You tell Mrs. Drummond to get her own dog."

"I will, Kyle."

"You tell Mrs. Drummond she can't have Dudley."

"Yes, Kyle. I promise I will."

Kyle turned around and stomped all the way upstairs with Mutley and Dudley following behind. She could hear him talking himself down from his angry place. Why didn't she listen to Lincoln on this one? Groaning, Maddie grabbed a bottle of water from the fridge and went outside. Sitting down on the steps, she viewed her surroundings.

The fields were due to be mowed soon. She had already called Rick, the farmer down the road who always hayed the fields for Daisy. He had no problem with continuing to hay for her, and the deal was he did the mowing and kept half the hay. She did not know anything about mowing, so she figured it was a good deal. Even if it was not a great deal, it was not likely she would ever learn to hay it herself or have the time.

Hearing the geese out back, Maddie stood up. Maybe a trip to the beach this afternoon would help soothe Kyle. He could bring Mutley and Dudley with him. And she could pack dinner for them. Upstairs she found Kyle's room empty. Calling his name, an uneasy feeling overcame her when there was no reply. Downstairs she checked every room.

Realizing the sound of the geese could have been Kyle going out the back door, Maddie went outside. Lucy and Ricky were about fifty feet away, picking through their feed dish. Kyle had to have come out and given them some food. Turning around, Maddie went to the barn and found it empty. All the animals were in their pens. The donkeys brayed when they saw her, probably in hopes she would stop to play.

Calling out Kyle's name again, she waited for any type of response from him. When there was none, Maddie followed the path out back. Looking at the grass, she did not see it had been disturbed. She was no tracker by any means, but she could tell nobody had come down the path in a long time. Running around the house, she ran into Lucy and Ricky on the other side waiting for her. Going to the can, she threw them some treats and ran down the path toward the beach.

"Kyle! Where are you?" Maddie yelled as she ran down the path. When she came around the corner to the sand, she looked up and down the beach. No Kyle or dogs in sight. Her heart pounded in her chest, and her breath came in short gasps. Turning around, she ran back toward the farm.

What ifs kept going through her mind. What if Kyle fell and got hurt? What if he had heart problems? While he had been to the doctors a week ago and passed his physical, she was still paranoid about his history. Wiping her face, Maddie kept running. Lucy and Ricky, seeing her coming, were ready, but they must have sensed something was off because instead of attacking, they ran the other way.

As she opened the door of the house, she yelled Kyle's name, but again was greeted with silence. Grabbing her phone off the dining room table, she dialed Lincoln's number. When it went right to voice mail, she took a deep breath.

"Lincoln, call me. Kyle's missing. I talked to him about Dudley, and I shouldn't have. Please call me as soon as you get this," she sobbed. Putting the phone into the pocket of her jeans, she went back out to the barn. Still no sign of Kyle. Sitting down on the ground in front of the doorway Maddie reached for her phone. Lincoln had not called back, and she debated whether to dial his number again. Only fifteen minutes had passed since she discovered Kyle missing but it felt like a lifetime.

All she could think about was what if something happened to him. She knew he was mad, but she thought she had calmed him down. The phone rang, and she swiped to answer it before she could even see who was calling. "Lincoln?" she asked.

"No, but I've got to meet this guy that leaves you out of breath like that," Kyra teased.

Maddie let a curse out before saying, "Kyra, I can't talk right now. Kyle's missing. I'll call you back later."

"I wanted to let you know I'm coming to see you," Kyra inserted just before Maddie hung up.

Before she could dial Lincoln's number again, it rang.

"Maddie, did you find him?"

"No. Can you help? It's all my fault, Lincoln. I should have listened…"

"I'll be there in ten." The phone call ended, and Maddie covered her face with her hands. She had really screwed up all the way around. Not just with Kyle, but with Lincoln, too. What if Lincoln gave up on her completely and did not want to be Kyle's social worker anymore? He could throw his hands up in the air and say he had enough. The thought scared her. There was no way she could have gotten as far as she did with the business or Kyle if Lincoln had not been beside her all the way.

Hearing a sound from inside the barn, Maddie stood up. Kyle was coming down the ladder, Mutley in his left arm, and Dudley on his back in the backpack with his little head peeking out. Holding her breath, she watched and waited, not wanting to startle him and have him lose his grip on the ladder.

As soon as his feet reached the floor of the barn, Maddie cried, "I've been looking for you everywhere. Didn't you hear me yelling your name?"

Kyle set Mutley on the floor and then took his backpack off so Dudley could get out. He looked at Maddie and smiled. "I went to my quiet place."

"But didn't you hear me yelling?"

"No, Maddie. I put my music on," he said and showed her the earplugs hanging from his neck.

"You scared me half to death. I didn't know where you were. I thought you ran away."

Kyle laughed. "I wouldn't run away. This is my home. You're silly sometimes, Maddie."

Maddie hung her head. "I'm sorry you got so upset about what I said about Mrs. Drummond. Can we make a deal, though? The next puppy comes along we will see if she wants it before we try to claim it as our own."

Kyle nodded. "It's a deal, Maddie. I'm hungry. I'm going to go get a snack."

As soon as Kyle went up the steps and into the house, Maddie heard Lincoln's truck in the driveway. After slamming on the brakes, he threw the door open and ran up to her.

"It's okay. I found him coming down the ladder in the barn. He just went in the house for a snack."

"Oh, thank God!" Lincoln said. "I can't tell you the things that went through my mind."

"You know, I probably had those same thoughts myself. What's this about his quiet place, as he called it? What's up there?"

"Hay. But Kyle's always used it as a place to hang out. I should have told you to look there."

"That would have been nice," she said. "I ran to the beach and back again in about five minutes."

"How is he? Still mad at you?" Lincoln asked.

Shaking her head, Maddie said the words she hated to say. "I'm sorry, Lincoln. You were right. I should have listened to you. He totally freaked out."

Lincoln leaned in closer. "No. You were right. In fact, I think I need to back off some and give you and Kyle more space. I think you guys can handle the chores together. You've got the hang of it."

"No, Lincoln. I mean, yes, we can handle the chores, but we…Kyle likes having you around." Maddie's tried to keep the panic out of her voice but was not sure if she succeeded or not.

"Yes, he does, but I was never around this much before Daisy passed. He will be fine. You'll see. And he will still see me a lot as I check up on him at work and meet with him once a week anyway."

"But…" Maddie tried to interject. Lincoln couldn't stop coming around altogether. Could he? *What about me?* The words almost came out of her mouth.

"You'll be fine. Tell Kyle I will see him on Monday." Lincoln turned to go back to his truck leaving Maddie alone in the barn.

Chapter Fifteen

Maddie set the shovel down and groaned. Kyle had already finished his chores for the morning and was inside eating a snack. She, on the other hand, was slow as cold molasses as her aunt would have told her. She still had to feed the chickens and check their water dishes. Then she could relax.

Relax—the thought made her laugh. Relaxing was something of the past. She could hire someone to help her around the farm. She could certainly afford it. But she did not want some stranger coming in to help. She wanted Lincoln. Tears in her eyes, she recalled how he had basically told her she was on her own from now on and how quickly he had left.

Kyle and she spent the evening talking about how they were going to respect each other's wishes and always let the other one know where they were going before they went anywhere. Hopefully, she had gotten through to him and made him understand she did not want him to give up Dudley—they just would not be able to keep any more animals that were found. Kyle agreed and they had spent the evening watching a movie. He had not asked where Lincoln was, and she did not volunteer any information.

At the sound of a car coming down the driveway Maddie peeked out the barn door. A black *Volvo* she had never seen before crept slowly down the driveway, and with tinted windows, she could not see who was driving. It stopped beside her car and the door opened. Maddie let out a squeal and went running from the barn.

"Kyra? What are you doing here?" Maddie threw her arms around her best friend who stood there with her arms up in the air.

"Maddie, back off for a second. You stink like…I don't know what you smell like, but it isn't good." Kyra wiped off the sleeves of her white top and inspected for any dirt.

Maddie laughed and jumped up and down. "Cut it out. It's only hay. I am so sorry I didn't call you back last night."

Kyra looked around at the farm. "Well, I can see why. This place is huge. I take it you found Kyle?"

"Yeah. He's fine. Come inside to meet him," she said. Then realizing she still had a couple of things to do, she glanced at Kyra in her sneakers. "Nope. Wait on that. I have one more thing to do, and you can come with me."

Kyra followed close behind, careful to not step in anything that might mess up her sneakers. "Maddie, what are you doing?" she groaned.

Laughing, Maddie resisted the urge to pick up some hay and throw it at Kyra. "I'm going to feed and water the chickens. Then we are going to collect the eggs."

"We? I don't think so," Kyra squealed.

"Then I'm going to show you the other animals. Follow me."

At the chicken coop, Kyra stood outside watching as Maddie fed and watered them. Then she motioned for Kyra to come inside. Kyra shook her head and remained outside.

"Kyra, I've never known you to back out of a dare. I dare you to come inside and get one egg," Maddie teased.

"Count me out on that dare. This is gross. There's chicken poop everywhere."

"Well, of course there is. Where else do you think they're going to poop?" Maddie yelled as she filled her basket with eggs. These would go right in the fridge. It amazed her how many people stopped by for a dozen of fresh eggs. They would leave the money in the cup and take what they needed. Kyle's chore was to collect the money and put it in the jar in the kitchen. When the jar was full, they would treat themselves to dinner. That would change, though, as she wanted every penny the farm earned to go into the bank account, allowing her to account for every bit the farm earned.

"How do you do this? I never pictured you as the farm girl type. Is this what you do all day? Clean up after animals?" Kyra's nose wrinkled, and she covered her mouth.

"Nope. There is a lot more than this to do. I also take Kyle to and from work, milk the goat, gather…"

"Milk the goat? Why? That is disgusting."

Maddie came out of the chicken coop carrying the basket of eggs. "You know the mask I sent you? That is why. I made a lotion with it, too."

"Yeah, but…"

"No such thing as a yabbit, Kyra." Maddie smiled. Those were the words her Aunt Daisy used on her.

"I get it, but are you really happy here? I miss you in Boston. We don't even get to talk that much on the phone." Kyra pouted and gave Maddie the look she had used over the years to get her way.

Before Maddie could respond the sound of a vehicle had them looking toward the driveway. When she saw Lincoln's truck, her stomach churned. She watched as he got out and looked toward the barn. When he saw her at the chicken coop, he waved and started walking her way.

"Who is that? Is that Lincoln? No wonder you like it here."

Maddie's eyes never left Lincoln, but she did respond to Kyra in a plea. "Please don't say anything stupid. Keep your thoughts to yourself, please."

"Oh, leave it to you to take the fun out of it." Kyra laughed. "Holy hotness. That man is good looking."

Lincoln nodded to Kyra, and then looked at Maddie. "Sorry to interrupt, but I wanted to drop the feed off to you. I forgot to get it out of the back of the truck last night."

Maddie straightened her shoulders. "Great. Thanks. Oh, and this is Kyra. She's been my friend since…well, forever."

"Hey, Lincoln. I was telling Maddie how I don't picture her as a farm girl, but I am beginning to see it now." Kyra offered her hand to Lincoln to shake, and then turned to smirk at Maddie.

Maddie rolled her eyes. "Oh, stop. Do you want some help unloading the truck? I am sure Kyra would love to get a workout in this morning."

Kyra grinned. "Oh, I'd rather sit back and watch."

Lincoln grinned at both of them and turned to walk back toward the truck. Maddie grasped Kyra by the arm and squeezed. "Stop it. Lincoln and I had a falling out last night. I don't need you to make it worse."

Pulling her arm away, Kyra whispered, "Why? What happened?"

"I'll tell you later. Let's do this, okay? Just behave," Maddie warned.

Behave was a word Kyra did not know, and she took it upon herself to give Lincoln the third degree. What irritated Maddie was the huge grin on Lincoln's face as he answered her questions. Yes, Kyra was beautiful, but Lincoln did not have to act like he had never seen a beautiful woman before. And Kyra did not have to flirt so outrageously, either. By the time the bags were stacked in the barn, Maddie was fuming at them both. But she managed to hold it in, giving them a smile when necessary, and pretending everything was okay.

"Lincoln, are you going to stick around for lunch? I wanted to take Maddie out to lunch today and we'd love for you to join us," Kyra asked, and Maddie flinched.

"Um, thank you, but why don't I see if Kyle wants to hang out with me today and you guys can spend some time together. I'm sure you've got a lot to catch up on," he replied, but his eyes wandered to Maddie when he said it.

Grateful Lincoln would offer, especially after last night, Maddie asked, "Do you mind? I'm sure Kyle doesn't want to hang out with us. But Kyra just got here and hasn't even had a chance to meet him yet. Would you be willing to come back in about an hour? That way I can ask Kyle what he wants to do first. If he wants to stay here, I can call you."

After agreeing to a time to pick up Kyle, Lincoln drove off, giving Maddie a chance to scold Kyra.

"Did you hear what I said? Lincoln and I had words last night and now you invite him to lunch?"

Kyra shook her hair out and inspected her nails. "Well, you obviously like him. I thought it would be nice to get to know the guy you're going to marry."

"I'm warning you right now. Do not say anything like that around Kyle. He hates change, and I don't want him getting upset over nothing. Got it?" she asked, pointing her finger at Kyra's chest.

"Got it, Farm Girl," Kyra replied as she sauntered toward the house with Maddie on her heels.

***

"Kyle, can you come downstairs for a minute?" Maddie then whispered to Kyra, "He spends a lot of time with his dogs."

Kyra glanced around the kitchen and the dining room and spotted Jake in the living room. At that moment, Peaches came out of the living room, barking at unexpected company. Kyra raised her eyebrows. "My God, how many dogs are there?"

Maddie laughed and scooped up Peaches in her arms. "We have six now. Lily and Bella are in the living room, this is Peaches, that's Jake, and Mutley and Dudley are upstairs with Kyle." Turning to the staircase, she yelled again, "Kyle? Can you please come down here?" She waited until she heard his door opening and then turned back to Kyra. "He's a sweetheart. Just be careful of what you say, please."

When Kyle stepped into the dining room, Kyra spoke before Maddie could. "Hi Kyle. I'm Kyra, Maddie's friend from Boston."

Kyle glanced to Maddie and then back at Kyra. "Nice to meet you." He then pointed to the floor and said, "That's Mutley and that's Dudley."

"Well, they are almost as cute as you are," Kyra teased.

Maddie cringed. What on earth was Kyra doing? Kyle wasn't two-years-old. She did not need to speak to him like he was a child.

"Kyle, since Kyra came for the day, Lincoln wants to know if you want to go hang out with him instead of us." Maddie watched relief sweep over Kyle's face.

"I want to go with Lincoln."

"Awe, dude! You don't want to hang out with me?"

Put in the spotlight, Kyle's face turned red. He then looked at his dogs and said, "Come on Mutley. Come Dudley." Maddie could not make out what he was saying, but he was muttering to himself all the way to his room. She couldn't blame him.

"Kyra, you can't speak to him like he is a child. He's twenty-years-old."

"I wasn't, was I?" Regret showed on Kyra's face.

"Yeah, you kind of were. But it's okay. Kyle is very forgiving. Now tell me, what are you really doing here?" Maddie asked as she poured a cup of coffee for each of them.

Sitting at the kitchen table Kyra picked up the chicken saltshaker. "Is this what you really want, Maddie? I mean…look at this place. This isn't you. A chicken saltshaker?"

Maddie's shoulders slumped. She should have figured Kyra would show up and beg her to come back. For the last twenty years they had been inseparable. They had so many plans together. They were going to marry friends and raise children together. First, though, they were going to conquer the corporate world. Kyra in real estate and she in marketing.

"I'm sorry, Kyra. Life changes. I didn't plan on this, but I can't back out of it. Kyle is the only family I really have left."

Kyra slumped in the worn-out chair. Leaning forward she placed her head in her hands and tears welled in her eyes. "It's not the same without you in Boston. I pick up the phone all the time to call you to see if you want to do something. I forget you're not there anymore."

Maddie's eyes filled with tears. She then grinned at Kyra. "But at least we're only a few hours apart. You can come on the weekends."

Kyra giggled. "I'm not like you, Maddie. Look at how well you have adapted. I can honestly tell you how thankful I am that I am leaving later today. Chickens. Cows. Donkeys. You can keep them. But I do want you to think about something. How would Kyle do if you moved him to Boston?"

Maddie inhaled. Kyle in Boston? "No, Kyra. This farm is his home. I could never take it away from him even if were a possibility. As part of the agreement, we have to live on the farm."

"You do realize that if you wanted to go back to Boston you could still be a part of his life, don't you?"

"I thought about that. When I first got here, I felt so out of place. I haven't exactly made all the right decisions regarding Kyle, which is why me and Lincoln clashed about a few things. But…no, I couldn't leave him unless I thought it was better for him. Right now, we seem to be doing surprisingly good. He really is a sweetheart."

Kyra sighed. "I'm not going to change your mind, am I?"

Maddie shook her head and took a sip of her coffee. No, she was in this for the long haul. Or at least that was what she wanted. Didn't she?

***

Maddie put the last of the dishes in the cupboard as Lincoln's truck came into view. Kyra had left about a half-hour ago leaving her mentally exhausted. Kyra meant well, but all the nagging and begging her to come back to Boston had left her in a sour mood. Had she made the right choice? Time would tell, she guessed.

Kyle came through the door first and looked around the kitchen. "Is she gone?" he asked.

Maddie laughed loudly. "Yeah. She went back home a little while ago."

Kyle smiled and said, "She's weird."

Maddie nodded, and Lincoln, who came through the door right behind Kyle, grinned. "She certainly is, Kyle, but that's why I love her so much."

Kyle went to the refrigerator, opened the door, and looked inside. "Can I have something? I'm starving. Me and Lincoln worked hard today."

"What did you guys do?" She watched the exchange of looks between them. Grabbing the pot from the coffee maker, she filled it in the sink.

"We went mountain climbing, Maddie. I'm starving." Kyle rummaged through the fridge and brought out a container of fruit. "Can I eat this?"

"Go ahead. I know it's past supper, but do you want a sandwich?" she asked.

Shaking his head, Kyle grabbed a spoon and sat down at the table. She watched as he ate quickly. "Sounds like you guys had a great day," she said. To Lincoln, she said, "Thank you for doing this. Kyra's visit was a little unexpected."

"That's alright. I had planned to go hiking anyway. Kyle was good company." Reaching down, he petted Peaches who had come out to greet everyone. Upon seeing Maddie, she went over and plopped down on the rug by her feet.

"I'm going up to see Mutley and Dudley. Thank you for a great day and keeping me away from the weird girl," Kyle said, and disappeared up the stairs.

Both Lincoln and Maddie smiled. Maddie knew Kyle was right. Kyra was different, but that was why they were friends. Kyra brought out the best in Maddie. She made her have fun even when she wanted nothing more than to be left alone. If Kyra had not been around when she lost her sister, and then her father and mother, Maddie did not know what she would have done.

"Well, I'm off. I will stop by and see Kyle at work tomorrow. You have a good week," Lincoln said as he turned for the door.

"Uh…thank you again, Lincoln. Do you want a cup of coffee before you leave?" Maddie turned on the coffee pot and turned to face him.

"No, I'm good, and I've got a few things to do. But thank you for the offer."

Watching him leaving in his truck, Maddie scowled. It was obvious Lincoln meant what he said last night. He was backing off, and she really could not blame him. She had been needy with him right from the beginning, and if she had learned one thing about men in her twenty-nine years, it was that men did not like needy women. Taking the last sip from her coffee cup, Maddie put it on the counter and went out to do the evening chores. She would not bother Kyle with them tonight. After all, everyone needed a day off occasionally.

Chapter Sixteen

It was a warm summer day, and Maddie had taken some time to herself after dropping Kyle off to work. The beach had been relaxing. The only sounds she heard had been the seagulls and an occasional lobster boat off in the distance. After a few hours, though, she could not take the quiet anymore and went back to the farmhouse. With a few hours left before she had to pick up Kyle, she decided to read more of her aunt's journal.

Still finding it difficult her aunt had been alive all these years, Maddie loved reading her words. Some days it made her feel closer to her and other's, it gave her perspective on dealing with Kyle and the farm.

January 1

Today is the first day of the New Year and I am grateful for whatever it may hold. Besides my blood pressure, I'm healthy, and I guess you could say I'm happy. If I died tomorrow, I'd die happy. My only fear is what will become of Kyle should something to happen to me. Yes, I have a will. The farm will go to whoever will agree to take care of Kyle. My Madelyn is first on the list, but my problem is who is second? What if Madelyn chooses to continue her life in Boston? She has a career. Would she be willing to give it all up for Kyle?

Maddie smiled. She had given up her life in Boston, and she still could not believe it had been such a difficult decision for her to make. Life on the farm was far from boring. The animals, who she had grown quite attached to, kept her busy, and she had expanded her aunt's business enough that she thought would make her aunt proud. No, she was not distributing to large stores yet, but it could happen.

January 3

After taking the day off to reflect on the situation with Kyle, I have decided to name Lincoln Davies as the next person on the list. A great human being with a big heart, Lincoln would do his best to make sure Kyle's needs are met. Yes, Kyle needs family, but most important, he needs someone who truly cares about his well-being. Am I making a mistake to put Madelyn's name first? Maybe. I'm going to have to think on that some more. But for now, I feel better that I have another name on the list. There are a couple more I will put down, but only as a backup plan. Not that I expect anything to happen to me. I'm a tough old broad and don't plan on going anywhere too soon.

Maddie closed the journal. Her aunt had not thought she would care about Kyle enough to leave Boston? Her aunt thought Lincoln was the better choice? Letting out a breath, she set the journal down on the bed with shaky hands. She could not help the tears forming and wiped at them in anger. She thought her aunt had chosen her because she believed she would do great with Kyle and the business. To find out she thought Lincoln would be better for Kyle hurt more than she ever could have imagined.

After placing the journal back in the bookcase, Maddie went to her room. She had made it her own, replacing the old, worn bedding with her own. She had hung up her curtains, wall decor, and put down the rug she had paid too much for in Boston. The room looked like hers now and like they belonged. But did she?

***

Kyle came home in a mood similar to her own. She could tell it would be a rough evening when he got in the car and slammed the door without any word of greeting. Normally, he came out smiling.

"Hey, Bud. You okay?" she asked and put the car in gear to back out.

"I'm fine. Just fine," he answered quickly. He then muttered to himself, "Kyle is fine. Kyle is fine."

"Okay. Well, let's get home then. I am making spaghetti and garlic bread for dinner tonight." No response from him so she was quiet the rest of the trip home. It was not until she mentioned chores that Kyle snapped.

"Put the items in the bag, Kyle. Do your chores, Kyle. Everyone always tells me what to do," he yelled and stomped up the stairs to his room.

Maddie put on her boots and grumbled, "This is not what I needed today. He had a bad day? What about me? Nope, you don't matter. You got to go out and do the chores by yourself tonight."

Peaches whined at her feet and Maddie softened. "It's okay, girl. I'm not mad at you. Just mad at myself, I guess. I thought I could do this, but things are getting a little out of control." Petting the dog on the head, Maddie

165

whispered, "I'll be back in a bit. I'm going to start on the chores, and then I'll be in to make dinner."

***

An hour later Maddie found herself stirring the sauce on the stove and feeling even more despondent. Something had to get her out of this funk, or she would soon be packing her bags to leave. She hated feeling that way but did not want to be the one to hold Kyle back from having a good life. While they had made some great memories, most of the time he was unhappy. Maybe this time his job was the cause of it, but usually it was her.

Calling him down when dinner was ready, Maddie prepared herself. Kyle bounced down the steps with a smile on his face. Maddie's smile did not quite make it to her face.

"Maddie, this smells good," Kyle stated and picked up the garlic bread.

"Thanks," she replied and sat down beside him at the table. She watched as he proceeded to eat, seemingly without a care in the world. Was it really this simple? He vocalized his displeasure and that was it? No grudges? An hour ago, he was mad at the world. What had changed?

When he was done, Kyle stood up and put his dishes away in the dishwasher. "I'm going to go do my chores."

Maddie knew she had to go help but could not seem to get the energy to get out of the chair. These ups and downs were exhausting. The problem was not so much with Kyle—she knew that. The problem was hers. Lifting herself from the chair she groaned. It was not only emotional exhaustion she felt. For a twenty-nine-year-old, she should not have felt that way.

It was not until Kyle went to bed that night that she was able to sit down in the office with Peaches at her feet. If she were to walk away from the inheritance it would not just be walking away from Kyle and the farm. Over the last few months, she had built up a fairly good clientele for the business. Would Lincoln be able to continue it? She doubted he would want to spend his time making skincare products for women or even jellies. It was part of Daisy's dream, too. That dream would probably go under.

But was the business worth the cost of Kyle's happiness? She did not believe her Aunt Daisy would think so. Kyle was her son. She wanted the best for him. And from the sound of what she had read Lincoln was best for Kyle. The only reason Daisy did not replace her name with Lincoln was because she was blood. But did blood really matter at this point?

As she saw the new list of orders received from the website, she could not help but worry. She had enough product to cover the orders, but she would need to make more this week. If she stayed. Those thoughts stayed with her all the way upstairs and when she crawled into bed.

***

Maddie pulled into a parking space directly in front of Sal's office. Taking a deep breath, she opened the door with trembling hands. She did not expect to be here, but she had to ask some questions. When Sal greeted her in the office with a smile, it only made her want to burst into tears.

Instead, she shook his hand and said, "I have a couple of questions for you."

"Come on in, Madelyn. I don't have a meeting for another hour. What can I answer for you?" Sal directed her to sit down in the chair in front of his desk as he slipped into the chair behind it.

"Well, I'm going to get right to the point. Things are not going as I thought they would. What would happen if I decided to turn the inheritance over to the next person on the list?"

Sal put the pen down on the desk he had picked up and leaned back in his chair. "Explain how things are not going as you thought they would."

Maddie played with the ring on her finger. "I know about Lincoln, Sal. I know he was next on the list."

"How did you find this out?"

"I read my aunt's journal. She stated very clearly she thought Lincoln would be the better choice."

"Now, Maddie, I doubt very much that is what she meant. Lincoln was the next name on the list, but you are the only family she had left. After what happened to your sister and parents, it was only right for her to choose you as Kyle's guardian." Sal's voice was soothing, and Maddie thought he might have been better suited as a therapist than a lawyer.

"I know I'm family, but it doesn't mean I am the one that's right for the job. I want to know what would happen if I changed my mind," she demanded.

"Well, there would be several things to consider. The amount of money spent between the time it was signed over to you and now would have to be determined, and you would probably be required to pay that back to the estate. Then…"

"I haven't spent anything out of the inheritance. The only money I have spent has been my own, so that wouldn't be a problem. In fact, I think I've added to the funds since revamping the Dandelion Farm products."

"I heard about that. My wife has done nothing but talk about the fancy lotion you've been making. She'll be sorry to see you leave if you choose to do so. The truth is we all will. Kyle means a lot to the people in this town, and you've saved him."

"What have I saved him from? Lincoln? Lincoln is way better for Kyle than I am."

Sal leaned forward in his chair. "Is that what you really think? Let me tell you this. Your aunt never would have placed Kyle in your care or even thought about it if she didn't think it was a good fit. Sure, in her journals she may have questioned her decision. It was a big decision. Who wouldn't? However, she never changed it once your name was put down to inherit her estate."

"Well, her doubt in choosing me is all right in her journals. And I don't think Kyle is happy," she added. "One day Kyle seems good and the next he's not. I know he has gone through a lot of changes, but I don't know how to deal with it. I'm struggling enough with all of the changes I've gone through. You know what? I used to dress up every day for work. Now I throw on the work boots and jeans that are stained with God knows what."

Sal laughed, and Maddie grew more frustrated. Obviously, Sal did not understand. Standing up, she demanded, "Can you at least start the paperwork or do whatever you have to do? In the event I change my mind regarding this, I will pay for your time. I will be in contact soon."

"Now Madelyn, don't leave upset. I will get things started for you. I hope you know I really do want you to put some more thought into this before you make a final decision."

Nodding her head, Maddie tried to smile. "Thanks. I appreciate that."

***

"What can I get for you, Maddie?" Delia asked.

"How about a small coffee to go? No; make it to stay. And I guess I'll have a muffin, too." Maddie surveyed the offerings under the glass counter and added, "Make that a blueberry muffin."

"Absolutely. Grab a seat anywhere, and I'll get you some coffee."

One lone couple sat at the table in the corner, and it looked like a serious discussion was taking place. Maddie turned around and then decided to sit herself at the counter.

"How are things going?" Delia asked. "Kyle doing okay?"

Maddie shrugged. "It's going. He seems good one day and then the next day is difficult. Same with me."

"Oh, honey, Daisy used to say the same thing. No twenty-year-old is always easy to deal with but it's worth it." Delia set Maddie's coffee down beside the muffin. "Kyle's a sweetheart."

"I know he is. It's not Kyle…really. I think someone else would be better for him. What do I know about farming? Or Down Syndrome? Maybe someone else could do a much better job and make Kyle happier."

Delia laughed. "I call BS. Look what you've done with the farm. I have heard so much talk around town about lotions and face masks that its crazy. Keep doing what you're doing, and you'll be fine. So will Kyle. And, if you want to learn more about Down Syndrome, get Lincoln to set you up with some of the organizations around here. I know there are fundraisers every year. If you can network with other people who have children with Down Syndrome, you might feel a little more confident."

"I know, but Lincoln…"

"What about Lincoln? He's our town's most eligible bachelor and he's got eyes for you," Delia laughed. "But instead of making enemies with some of the younger women in the town, you've won them over with lotions and masks."

"He has eyes for me?" she questioned. He did try to kiss her one time, but she did not think it was a big deal. Half the time she thought he did not like her. The other half? No. He was not serious about her—not like Delia thought. But they had become good friends. Or at least she thought they had. She really missed having him around all the time. Dinner was a lot more fun when Lincoln was sitting at the table with them. And she missed the nights they would watch television together—completely comfortable with the silence between them.

"Oh yes. I can see it." Delia leaned over and refilled Maddie's cup. "It's too bad you can't. Now I've got to get some things done, but I'll stop by the farm soon and check out what you're doing. I think I need some of the lotion everyone's raving about."

***

Maddie sat down on the ground, and both Elsa and Anna immediately climbed into her lap. Bringing them close to her chest, Maddie relaxed. Two months ago, she never would have thought she would be sitting in dirt, playing with baby goats while the mother rummaged around for food a few feet away. No. Two months ago she was sitting at her desk, wearing her fancy clothes and shoes, trying to lure in a new client.

One of the kids reached up and started to chew on her hair. Two months ago, it would have disgusted her. Now, she found it endearing. But it was not about her renewed love of animals. This whole situation was about Kyle. What made her think she could provide what he needed? Lincoln was a social worker who had been working with people with special needs his whole life. He was better equipped to give Kyle the life he deserved. She was not.

Chapter Seventeen

Sitting down beside Kyle at the table, Maddie glanced over at him as he took a bite of the quiche she made for dinner. Scrunching his nose up, Kyle shook his head. "Not good, Maddie. Not good."

"But you like eggs."

"Not good," was his response, and he put his fork down on the table.

"Well, what would you like then?" she asked.

"Pizza."

"No. We just had pizza the other day. You want a salad? Leftover spaghetti?"

"Pizza."

"Kyle, I don't have any pizza. What else would you like?" she repeated.

Kyle raised his voice. "I don't want nothing else. I want pizza."

Frustrated now, Maddie looked at Kyle in his eyes. "I know you want pizza, Kyle. We do not have any. If you do not like the quiche, I will make something else quick. But it is not going to be pizza." Her voice was calm but stern.

Kyle stood up and walked to the stairs. All the way to the top, she heard him muttering, "No pizza for you, Kyle. No pizza for you."

Maddie laid her head on the table and groaned. She had expected a temper tantrum to ensue. Thankfully, Kyle was working to control himself. Knowing Kyle, he would be back down soon to get something out of the refrigerator.

After cleaning up the mess from dinner, Maddie quickly did the evening chores. Kyle was still up in his room, and Maddie did not bother to ask him for help. After being here this long, she could easily get the last chores of the day done with ease. After saying goodnight to all the animals, Maddie went inside. She still had to finish cleaning out her aunt's room. She would not leave that for someone else. That thought made her sigh, as she really had not made up her mind.

She would call Kyra to talk with her about it but realized Kyra would not really help her. She would probably see it as an opportunity to convince her to leave. Maddie knew she had to make up her mind quickly. She had already told Sal to get the paperwork ready. Now she had to make the decision. She had asked herself a hundred times what she wanted. The truth was she did not know. She loved it here, but it was Kyle's well-being that mattered. Not hers. She would have to rethink employment as there was no way Wendy would hire her back, and if word got out from the Blue Market Brothers, she would not have a job in marketing anyway.

When she made it upstairs, she did not hear any sound from Kyle's room. However, by the mess left on the counter in the kitchen, she assumed he had made himself a sandwich. In her aunt's room she went to the closet. Several boxes were stacked to the side. Pulling them out, she opened the first to discover it was filled with her aunt's old journals.

Grabbing the first one on the top, Maddie leaned back and opened it.

December 24, 2001

It is hard to believe I am celebrating this Christmas with a baby. I never believed I'd have one of my own and, honestly, I would have been just fine with that. But the Good Lord provides and that is what he did.

Of course, Kyle isn't the easiest. There are days that boy is so fussy that I have to just let him cry it out or I wouldn't get anything done. I'm just glad that he's here. I can't imagine that woman would have had the patience to raise a child like Kyle. Like I said, the Good Lord provides.

Skipping back several pages, Maddie continued reading.

September 4, 2001

Still hard to believe that I get woken up every morning with cries of hunger. From what the doctors stated, they doubted that Kyle would cry at all. Evidently, they thought he would curl up and suffer silently until he took his last breath. Not on my watch. I promised her that I would raise him with love and cherish every moment with him and that's what I'm going to do until she comes to her senses and comes to help.

Maddie did not realize she had been holding her breath until she found her chest ready to explode. So, whoever Daisy adopted Kyle from was going to come help? Why couldn't she help when he was born? What type of mother would pawn her child off on someone else? And why did Daisy promise to do this?

Flipping back further, Maddie picked a date a few weeks prior.

August 20, 2001

I have never been more thankful in my life than I am today. I am thankful for whatever time God gives us with this young child. I am thankful for God being there for this young woman and making it easier for her. Poor Phoenix is going to need a lot of love and support and I hope God can provide it to her. Right now, Lord, I need forgiveness for what I'm thinking. I'd like nothing more than to wrap my hands around my sister's neck and...see Lord, I need forgiveness for even thinking this. While Phoenix is hurting, all her mother can think about is what other people are going to think. Who cares what others think? I said that to her, and she just slammed down the phone. Conversation over. Well, let me tell you, I'm not sure what she is going to say when she hears what was decided with Kyle. I'm going to take him in and raise him as my own. I'm adopting him and when his mother is ready to be a part of his life, she'll be welcome. Right now, it's just too darn complicated for a sixteen-year-old to figure out.

What the heck did Phoenix have to do with all of this? Why would she need love and support and why would Aunt Daisy be mad at her sister? Sixteen-year-old? Maddie's eyes widened. Did this mean what she thought it meant? Did Phoenix give birth to Kyle? Maddie could not breathe. Was this why Phoenix went away for the whole summer? Is this why she did not get to come that summer?

Wiping at tears rolling down her face, Maddie sat down on the edge of the bed. How on earth could this have happened, and she had never known a thing about it? She had only been nine, but her parents should have told her something. Phoenix should have said something…anything…to her.

Thinking back, she recalled how Phoenix had come back quiet. She had screamed at her big sister, mad she didn't get to go to the farm for the summer.

"Thanks a lot Phoenix. You're so selfish and mean. Why would you do this? I wanted to go, too, but no…you are so selfish. I'm never speaking to you again!" she'd yelled.

Phoenix had simply stared at her, not saying a word. After a few moments, she went upstairs to her room and locked herself inside. Not even one word to her. They barely spoke after that.

Was this secret what changed Phoenix? Phoenix and she had once been close. Well, even though they were several years apart, Phoenix had enjoyed spending time with her. After she had come back at the end of summer, though, there was nothing. Phoenix spent most of her time in her room and, when she did decide to become social again, she started hanging out with the wrong crowd.

Her parents and Phoenix argued a lot. It wasn't like anything before, either. Before she had gone away for the summer, her parents had argued 'nicely' with her about getting better grades or about curfew. After that summer, things had gone bad quickly. Maddie remembered her father yelling at Phoenix. *"How many more times are you going to screw up, Phoenix? How many more lives are you going to mess up?"*

Maddie leaned over feeling queasy. How could this have all happened? They had been such a normal family. Phoenix? Phoenix was Kyle's mother? Which made her Kyle's aunt? This was crazy. Maddie stood up and paced around the floor. How much of this did Kyle know? People in town? Lincoln?

Taking a deep breath, Maddie tried to focus. More than likely, nobody really knew what happened all those years ago. She did not know why it really mattered anyway. It was not like she was at fault for anything that happened all those years ago. She had only been nine. If someone had told her what was going on, it was doubtful she would have understood it anyway.

August 22, 2001

I told my sister of my plans to adopt the baby when it was born, and she told me that I couldn't do it. When I asked her why not, she stated,"Because that baby will be dead to us. If you have it, you'll be dead to us, too." I never knew just how terrible my sister could be. Her words are hurtful. She told me I would never see Phoenix or Maddie again. Oh, my Madelyn! She was so hurt to not be able to come this summer, but her mother did not want her "tainted" by what Phoenix did. Oh Lord, I am just asking for strength to get me through this. I want to see those children again, but I cannot trade one child for another. If I don't keep this baby, who is going to raise him? He needs family, Lord. He needs me. And regardless of what Phoenix thinks right now, he is her son and someday she'll regret giving him away. At least this way, she'll know exactly where he is when she decides she can handle it.

The thought of Phoenix going through a pregnancy at such a young age and with no support from either of her parents left Maddie feeling uneasy. She had always known her parents were considered a little uptight, but many teenage girls had given birth in their school. No, it did not make it right, but for Phoenix to not get any support, it just seemed unbelievable.

But then again, Maddie remembered several mornings before school where there were big arguments about what Phoenix could wear that day. Anything above the knee and her father would go ballistic. Of course, after Phoenix died, they didn't really care what she wore. She could have gone to school in a mini skirt barely covering anything and her father would have not even given her a second glance.

Even her mother did not pay attention to her after Phoenix had died. That made Maddie wonder if they had felt guilty. Would Phoenix have died if she had been allowed to keep her child? Did she even want to keep her child? And who was the father?

That last question seemed like it might have been the most important thing. Kyle probably had a father out there that did not know he existed. At nine-years-old, she did not even know what dating was let alone know who Phoenix had been seeing and, if she had known, it was long forgotten.

***

With her mind whirling with all the newfound information, Maddie dialed Kyra. She might not know anything about this, but Kyra could get information on anything and anyone. Maddie always joked with her that she was the 'busy-body' of the neighborhood—even as a kid.

"It's about time you called," Kyra stated. "What is going on? Are you coming back to Boston?"

"I don't know what I'm doing. But I have to talk to you. Kyle is not just Aunt Daisy's adopted son. He's my nephew."

"What? A nephew? You don't have a nephew!"

"I just found out. Long story short, I found my Aunt Daisy's old journals. Everything is in there. My sister gave birth to him when she was sixteen. My aunt adopted him, and my parents told me my aunt was dead. Why? I have no clue. What am I going to do?"

There was silence for a few seconds before Kyra spoke. "Maddie, I'm going to have to sit down for this one. Phoenix had a baby at sixteen? I don't get it. Why didn't you know about this?" Kyra asked.

Maddie's voice trembled. "I don't know. I don't know why they kept this from me, except I was only nine. Other than that, I don't know. I came here believing Kyle was her adopted son…not my actual blood."

"Oh my God, Maddie! What are you going to do?"

"What matters is trying to figure out what I'm going to do about Kyle. I was getting ready to pack my bags when I found Aunt Daisy's journals. If it were the farm only, it wouldn't be a big deal. But with Kyle, it's a whole different story." Maddie sat down and rested her head in her hands.

"Do you remember anything at all about Phoenix? Like who she might have been dating when she got pregnant? I can't remember a thing about that time."

Maddie viewed herself in the mirror above her aunt's dresser. Her dark hair was pulled back in a haphazard ponytail and her face without makeup revealed the stress lines caused by her worry. Turning her back to the mirror, she added, "I don't even know if his biological father knows about him, Kyra. Can you imagine?"

Kyra hesitated before answering, "I don't know. That was so long ago. I do remember being at your house one day and your parents telling Phoenix she couldn't see that guy in the white truck anymore. Oh…what was his name? He lived over on Maple. His sister was a year ahead of us. Chris? No, Chase. That was it. Chase Johnson. He was good looking, but definitely too old for Phoenix."

Chase Johnson in the white truck. She remembered him. He used to come over a little early to pick up Phoenix and sit with her on the couch and watch television until Phoenix would come downstairs. Of course, that was only if her parents were not home. If they were home, he never came near. She remembered the time her parents came home early one day, and Chase had snuck out the back door. Phoenix had made her promise not to tell and had promised her she would clean her room if she did not tell.

"Kyra, thank you. I can't believe I forgot all about him. I wonder if he is Kyle's father. I wonder if he even knew about him." Maddie whispered, "What if he knew but he didn't care? To me, that seems the likely choice. He wasn't exactly a good guy."

"Maddie, that happens a lot. Not exactly uncommon, even twenty years ago."

"I know. I just…I just can't believe all of this happened and I had no clue about it."

"You feel bad, but you can't stay because you found out Kyle was Phoenix's son," Kyra snapped. More softly, she said, "You belong in Boston…with me."

"Kyra, I know this sucks, but it's not like I'm that far away. I can have Lincoln stay with Kyle some weekends and come to visit."

"So, how is Lincoln? I still can't believe he's a social worker. He should be a model," Kyra teased.

"A model? That's taking things a little far," Maddie snickered. "He's fine, I guess."

"Tell me and be honest. Are you interested in him?" Kyra's voice was serious, and Maddie wanted to scream. All Kyra thought about was finding the right guy, and it had to be a good-looking one. Unfortunately, most of her time had been spent trying to find Maddie the right one.

"Kyra, no. He's Kyle's social worker. I already told you that. It's not going to happen. He's just…just a friend."

"Why does it matter if he is Kyle's social worker? Is there some kind of written rule saying he cannot date his client's family member? I still think you should go for it."

"It matters, Kyra. I don't know why, but it does. I'll call you soon. See what you can find out about Chase Johnson for me."

"Will do, and go tell Lincoln I miss him already," Kyra teased before she hung up.

Chapter Eighteen

Maddie paced around the house, knowing she needed to read more in the journals. She still did not have all the answers she needed, but the thought of finding out more caused her even more anxiety. After pouring a cup of coffee, Maddie took a deep breath and climbed the stairs.

In her hands, she held the journal that held the secret of what happened. She had flipped through until she found the dates corresponding to her sister's last visit. Rubbing her chest, she opened the page and started to read.

June 28th

My dear Phoenix arrived today, and the fear in her eyes leaves me bewildered. I can't imagine what it would be like to be sixteen and with child. And she is doing this without any support from her parents. That sister of mine is always so worried about what other people with think. The only reason Phoenix is with me for the summer is so that no one will find out. With her being so tall, she does not have much of a baby bump, but soon it will show no matter how hard she tries.

Phoenix tells me she doesn't want to keep this baby, but I know in her heart she believes it to be the only option. Without her parent's support, she knows she can't do it. I plan on telling her that if she wants to keep this baby, I will help her. She could continue to live with me even after the baby is born. I would help her in whatever way I can. Hopefully, I can talk some sense into that girl before she does something she will regret.

Maddie took it all in. She could imagine what Phoenix's pregnancy did to her mother. Her mother was…well, how could she put it? Uppity? Snobby? No, that was not entirely right. She never wanted anyone to see that her family was anything other than perfect—which was why her mother hated it when Aunt Daisy came to visit. Daisy would be outside chatting it up with neighbors, never caring if she let it slip that she and her sister came from a poor family that could barely scrape up enough to eat and keep shoes on their feet.

Every time Daisy came to visit, the two ended up fighting. Maddie was not sure if it was because Daisy let family secrets slip out or that all of their neighbors loved visiting with her when she was here.

June 29th

I swear that niece of mine is just as stubborn and stuck-up as that sister of mine. She is determined to put this baby up for adoption and knowing that this child will be born with special needs just makes her more adamant about adoption. All she cares about right now is making sure that nobody in her town finds out that she is pregnant. I asked her if the boyfriend knew, and she nodded her head and told me that he didn't want any baby either.

My heart breaks for my niece, knowing that someday when she gets older, she will regret giving this child up. A child with health problems is nothing to be ashamed of. Heck, in this day and age, an unplanned pregnancy is the norm. But, oh no, all Phoenix seems to care about right now is her. Yes, I know it's her age, but I still think she is too much like her mother. For now, all I can do is wait for this child to be born and see if she changes her mind.

Maddie wiped the tears from her eyes. When she first read Kyle belonged to Phoenix, her heart had cried out in sympathy for the older sister she had never really gotten to know. Now? She did not know how she felt. She was only twelve when her sister had been killed. She had been devastated. Her parents became zombies, doing only what was necessary. She had pretty much been on her own after that, and she had always felt selfish when feelings of anger and resentment overtook her.

Not sure if she wanted to continue to read or not, Maddie set the journal on her lap. She thought about how much Lincoln seemed to care about Kyle, and he was not even family. Kyle's own biological father did not want anything to do with him—or so it seemed. Lincoln was not like any man she had known. She only wished things could have been different between them. But like she had told Kyra, dating Lincoln did not seem like a good idea. And anyway, the men she dated wore business suits and shiny shoes. They would not be caught dead working on a farm.

Getting comfortable, she picked up the journal again and began reading.

July 1st

It's only been a few days, but my patience has worn thin already. Phoenix doesn't want to listen to a word the doctor says. She's drinking soda like there's no tomorrow and not caring what she puts into her body. I tried talking to her again about the baby, but it's no use. The hardest part for me is knowing that my great-nephew is going to be lost to me forever.

Part of me wants to offer to take the baby myself, but I'm no spring chicken. At forty years old, it would be ridiculous of me to even think about it. I always thought I'd have babies of my own, but it just never happened. After losing Ted, I didn't even look for another man. I didn't want another man. Ted was the only one for me.

However, I'm thinking that this little boy that is about to come into this harsh world might be the one for me, too. If my sister and niece don't want him, they shouldn't have a problem with me taking him. I may be forty, but I've always kept in shape. I just wonder if I'd be able to provide for a child with special need. He'll need surgery right away, they said. I just pray he makes it through.

Maddie put the journal down. Rubbing her temples, she closed her eyes. This whole thing was so overwhelming. She couldn't imagine how Kyle felt, knowing he was adopted. Kyle—her nephew. What she really wanted to know was why her aunt never contacted her, and she flipped through the journals until she came to the year of her mother's death.

At twenty, Maddie was still in college when her mother had passed. Her father's loss had hit her hard, but when her mother died, she was alone. Heartbroken over the deaths in her family, she now considered herself an orphan. If only she had known her Aunt Daisy was still alive. Would that have changed anything? Would she have left college and come to live in Maine if given the opportunity?

Finding the dates she was looking for, Maddie took a deep breath.

October 22nd,

My poor Madelyn! Her mother passed away yesterday, and I am torn. I do not want her to be all alone, but how can I tell her that I am still alive? How can I totally disrupt her life? She's got a 4.0 GPA, and if I come out of the woodwork and tell her what's been going on for the last eleven-years of her life, it's going to stress her out. Would she even finish college?

I miss my Maddie so badly. But that was the nine-year-old Maddie? She was the sweetest child. She loved animals, unlike her sister, and when she visited, it was all I could do to keep her from bringing her favorite chicken inside to sleep with her. She loved the farm. I wonder what she'd think of it now. I can guarantee she'd love the goats and donkeys. She'd probably be just like Kyle, outside every minute and wanting to baby every animal we brought in.

Am I selfish for wondering if she is too much like her mother and Phoenix before I get involved? God help me, I loved my niece and my sister, but I don't think I could deal with that kind of drama again.

Maybe I am just a coward but will send flowers anonymously. No need to upset her when she already has too much to handle.

October 24th,

Maddie let out her breath. Her aunt had thought she was like her mother and her sister. Daisy never contacted her because she did not want her around Kyle if she was like her mother. She wasn't! She was not like any of her family. She…Maddie hugged her legs close and rested her chin on her knees.

She was like her mother—at least in the beginning. Since finding out about Kyle, what had she done? In the beginning, she only thought about how her life would be affected if she accepted the inheritance. Yet, she had given little thought about Kyle. She thought about how tough it would be to run the farm. How nasty the animals were. Oh God, that really sounded like her mother! And, even worse, she had thought how difficult it would be to deal with Kyle. But she was not like that anymore.

Standing up, Maddie picked up the journals from the bed and placed them back on the small bookcase. She made up her mind. Now she had to see Sal in the morning and tell him to put a stop to the paperwork. She was not going to abandon her nephew.

Chapter Nineteen

Maddie had stepped out of her car after dropping Kyle off to work when she saw Lincoln's truck come barreling down the driveway. Dust flew in the air as he pulled up behind her car after slamming on the breaks. Panicking, Maddie ran to his window.

Lincoln's door opened and he stepped out. "Are you really going to leave Kyle? I spoke with Sal. What are you doing?"

Maddie froze. Sal already talked to Lincoln about taking over the farm? "Lincoln, let me explain. I…"

"No. I don't want your explanation. That boy has grown attached to you whether you believe it or not. He doesn't take to just anyone. Now you're going to walk out on him? I cannot tell you how disappointed I am. Honestly, I am disgusted." Lincoln got back in his truck, leaving Maddie standing there with her mouth open.

Maddie stood there for several minutes, unsure of what to even think. Anger toward Sal surfaced, and then disappeared. She had no one to be angry at but herself. Lincoln was right. Over the last few months, she and Kyle had developed a relationship—there were good days and bad— and she had been willing to throw it all away.

Things were different now. Kyle was her nephew— the only family she had left. She had wanted to call Lincoln last night, but she had put it off, wanting to talk to Sal first. Now she wished she had called him and filled him in about what she had found in the journals. Wiping at her face, Maddie breathed in slowly through her mouth and then out through her nose. First things first, she had to talk to Sal. She would worry about Lincoln afterwards.

Within an hour, after rushing through morning chores, Maddie found herself back in Sal's office. Instructed to sit down in the waiting area by the receptionist as Sal was in a meeting, Maddie sat down. Wringing her hands together she kept glancing at the clock above the receptionist's desk. After twenty-minutes had passed, she got up and asked, "Do you think Sal's going to be much longer? I really need to speak with him."

Before the receptionist could answer, the door to Sal's office opened and Lincoln stepped out.

"Lincoln, I need to talk to Sal, but can you wait for me?" Maddie blurted out.

"I've got a meeting," he said and then passed her, barely even glancing her way.

Sal stepped out and she could see the fatigue on his face. "Come in, Maddie."

Maddie quickly slipped into the chair and stated, "I'm not giving up Kyle, Sal. Before I explain, is everything I tell you going to be kept confidential? I need to make sure it is."

Sal straightened his shoulders. "Of course it is. I'm your lawyer. Everything in this office is held in strict confidence."

Maddie began speaking in a quiet voice. "I know I was in here about giving up Kyle and the inheritance, but I cannot do it. I recently found information that has…Kyle is actually my nephew. What I have to say can't be repeated to anyone. My aunt kept journals, and I went back and read them from when Kyle was born. When I was nine, my sister Phoenix came to stay with my aunt for the summer. That summer she gave birth to Kyle. My aunt was mad at her about giving the child up for adoption. Being that Kyle was her own blood, she decided to adopt him herself. My parents and Phoenix then decided my Aunt Daisy was dead to them. They wanted no contact with her after the adoption. That's when they told me my aunt died."

Sal leaned forward in his seat. "Oh, gosh. That certainly does change things, doesn't it?"

"It does. Should it, though? I was thinking about walking out on Kyle, but he was still my Aunt Daisy's son. Now I found out he is my blood. Should that change things? While it may not be right I thought about leaving, Kyle is my blood. Kyle really is the only family I have left, at least on my mother's side, and I'm not close to anyone on my father's. He's all I got," she said, grabbing a tissue from the box on the corner of the desk.

"Well, I cannot say how happy I am. I happened to run into Lincoln last night…"

Interrupting him, Maddie said, "Yeah, I heard all about it from Lincoln this morning after he ripped me a new one."

"Lincoln is a great advocate for his clients, Madelyn. Lincoln always puts his clients first. When Daisy died, I didn't even have to ask him to take over running the farm until you got here. Anything for Kyle. He cares a lot and that may be one of his biggest faults—but it's also his best quality."

Maddie agreed. "I get that. But now I have to work on repairing that bridge. I doubt he'll ever trust me again. Especially regarding Kyle, but I can tell you this. Kyle is loved. I guess I didn't realize I fell in love with him until I found out we are related by blood. The whole reason I was thinking about leaving was not about me. Well, to be honest, I didn't know how well I would handle the changes. I guess I should say the main reason I was thinking about leaving was I didn't think I was good enough for Kyle. Heck, I still might not be. But I'm going to do my best to make sure he's happy." Thinking back to his refusal to eat quiche, she added, "Happy but within reason. We don't need any more animals, and he cannot eat pizza every night."

Laughing, Sal picked up some paperwork off his desk and tore it in two. "I guess we don't need these then. You've made me a happy man today. Daisy was a wonderful woman. Eccentric, but things weren't always easy for her. When Ted died, she was lost. It was a rough time for her."

"Ted? I read about him in the journal. What happened?" Maddie had looked for his name in other journals but had yet to find anything on her aunt's past love.

Sal leaned back in his chair and his face became serious. "Ted was her fiancé. They bought the farm together and made all these plans for homesteading. Just before their wedding day, Ted died of an aneurysm. He and Daisy were building a chicken coop together and, suddenly, he dropped to the ground. It about killed her, too. But after a few weeks, she picked right up where they left off and continued living—on her own, though. However, when Kyle came along, it gave her someone to love her unconditionally as well. She's put that trust in you for a good reason, Maddie."

Maddie had never heard that story before. While it happened long before she was born, her parents never really talked about her aunt in front of her. The truth was she really did not know much about her aunt. Only that she loved her, and that love had always been returned.

Maddie leaned in and placed both hands on the desk before standing up. "I had no idea. Poor Aunt Daisy. I promise you, Sal, the only reason you'll see me again is to ask you to look over contracts for the business. I'm staying for good. Now I got to go find Lincoln and see if I can repair any damage that's been done."

Chapter Twenty

Maddie packed the picnic basket with fried chicken she had bought at the market. While she was expanding her culinary abilities, fried chicken was a little much to take on in August. The temperatures had been steadily in the eighties, and it was taking a toll on both she and Kyle. Chores in the heat became impossible, and the animals needed extra water which put a physical strain on both of them. Tonight, she was going all out to relax, though. Tonight, she and Kyle were having a picnic on the beach.

While there was a good cause to celebrate—she was staying in Cove's Port—Kyle would never know she was not just his caretaker cousin from Boston. She was his aunt. His biological aunt. She was his Aunt Maddie, and she would do everything possible to make sure he knew how much she loved him.

"We're ready, Maddie." Kyle stood at the bottom of the steps with both Mutley and Dudley at his feet. He wore a white t-shirt and his blue swimming trunks. She was wearing a white tank top and jean shorts with her bathing suit underneath, prepared to take a dip in the ocean with him.

"I'm ready, Kyle. I'll carry the basket if you take care of Lucy and Ricky. I'm too hot to run today," she said.

"Lucy and Ricky are nice, Maddie," Kyle scolded her. "You have to get to know them better."

"Yeah, well, all they want to do is chase me."

Kyle laughed and went out the door with his two dogs following close behind. Grabbing the basket, Maddie walked and waited until Lucy and Ricky were under Kyle's spell before she took the lead in the walk to the beach. Once they arrived, she spread out the blanket she had brought and set the basket down.

Out on the Atlantic, she could see a couple of sailboats. The water was calm with gentle waves lapping at the shore. Leaning back on her hands, she watched as Kyle and the dogs played at the edge of the water and smiled. She had been here two months and had not taken advantage of this nearly enough. The beach was important to Kyle, and she could see why. Sitting here it seemed like time did not matter. The only thing that mattered was happiness and the connection she was making with her nephew.

Maddie, engrossed in her thoughts, failed to see Kyle walking further down the beach. Hearing Kyle's yell for help, she jumped to her feet, her heart pounding.

"Maddie! Quick! Quick!" he yelled.

Running as fast as she could, worried something happened to either Kyle or his dogs, Maddie stopped short when she saw what Kyle was looking at. A small seal, most likely a pup, lie on the beach in front of Kyle. As she got closer, she could see it was alive, but obviously in trouble.

"It needs help, Maddie," Kyle whined.

"I know, buddy. I just have to figure out who to call. We're not supposed to touch them. Can you get Mutley and

Dudley and tie them to the driftwood over by our basket? I think they are scaring it.”

Grabbing her phone, Maddie searched and found the number to call for help. After explaining to the person on the other end what they had found, Maddie hung up and backed away from the seal. Help was on the way. Instructed to stay at least a hundred and fifty feet away from it, she went back to where Kyle had finished up securing the two dogs.

“Someone is on their way, Kyle. It’s a rescue group of volunteers who specialize in helping seals, so they will know what to do with this baby. They said we have to stay away from it but call them back if it returns to the water. In the meantime, why don’t we eat? They know how to get down here and I even warned them about Lucy and Ricky.”

“Okay, Maddie.” Kyle sat down on the blanket and reached into the basket. Pulling out a water, he took a drink. Grinning, he said, “You’re the best, Maddie.”

Maddie’s hand froze over the top of the basket and she looked at Kyle. “Awe, thank you. But you’re the best.”

Kyle laughed and picked up a piece of the fried chicken. It did not take long to finish the dinner and Maddie glanced at her watch and then at the path leading down to the beach. Seeing the top of a head coming down through the trees, Maddie stood up and wiped the sand from her legs. She was surprised to recognize Lincoln walking toward them. As soon as Kyle saw Lincoln, he yelled, “Lincoln. Come see the seal!”

“That’s why I’m here, Kyle.” He walked past Maddie and she found it difficult to take a breath. Then she realized what he said and took off after him.

"Wait, Lincoln. You rescue seals?" she asked.

"I'm a volunteer. I'm just going to assess the situation, see if it's in trouble. If it is, I'll take it to the rescue where they will see to its needs and release it when it's ready."

When they came within range of the seal pup, Lincoln told them to stay back. Maddie watched as he leaned in close and could hear his soft murmuring to the seal. *He really is a kind soul*, she thought. His love for all things living astounded her. It was just who he was.

Within a minute, Lincoln was back. To Kyle, he said, "Did you find the seal?" and then watched as Kyle nodded his head. "Good job. And great job for keeping the dogs away. Unfortunately, he does look like he's in distress. I have no idea what happened, but I'm going to get him to the rescue facility. They'll figure out what's wrong with him. But I need you guys to stay back. I'm going to cover his eyes and get him wrapped up before I carry him back up the path."

Maddie and Kyle both watched Lincoln from a distance and then as he carried the poor seal pup past them. As he was walking away, Maddie called out, "I need to talk to you as soon as you get a chance."

Lincoln waved his hand and kept walking. Both watched until he was out of sight and then Maddie asked, "You want to take a quick dip before we go back to the house?"

Kyle nodded and then untied the dogs. He pulled off his t-shirt. Maddie did the same and followed Kyle and his dogs to the water. They splashed and chased each other, but all Maddie could think about was how much fun it was when Lincoln was here the last time with them.

***

Maddie watched as Kyle came around the corner, almost running to her. "Maddie, Lincoln said the seal is going to be okay."

"Awe, that's great, Kyle. I'm glad to hear that," she replied dryly. It was hard to show any excitement regarding Lincoln as he had been ignoring her calls all day. After the third time calling him and getting his voice mail, she gave up.

"Lincoln said it was only a few months old. Lincoln said it weighed forty-eight pounds, but it wasn't enough. Lincoln said they have to feed it a lot," he said as he hooked up his seat belt.

Lincoln this. Lincoln that. Maddie was getting tired of his name, but she smiled and told Kyle how great Lincoln was for helping to rescue seal pups. Her irritation with Lincoln was growing by the hour. Yes, she may have been wrong for even thinking about leaving Maine and leaving Kyle behind, but Lincoln was pushing it. He should at least give her a chance to explain.

Not wanting any trouble at mealtime tonight, Maddie told Kyle he could choose what they had for dinner as long as it was not pizza. While pizza had always been a favorite, having it more than once a month was a little much for her.

"I don't know," was the reply she got.

"How about we grill some turkey burgers and veggies? It will be good." Receiving a head nod from Kyle, Maddie relaxed and drove the rest of the way in silence.

Seeing Lincoln's truck in the driveway caused Maddie to gulp. Pulling into the space she had claimed as her own, she shut the engine off. Kyle got out of the car, yelled, "Hi Lincoln," and ran for the house.

Maddie leaned down and grabbed her purse and checked the car for anything else she had to bring into the house. Lincoln leaned on his truck watching her. Taking a deep breath, Maddie opened the door. Time to face him and have her say. She only hoped he would listen to what she had to say and stop being so darned stubborn.

"Hey," was all she could manage to begin.

Lincoln crossed his arms over his chest, but never said a word.

Crossing her arms over her chest, as well, Maddie took a stance in front of him. "Okay. I get it. You're mad at me. I don't blame you. I wasn't thinking straight when I thought about leaving, and I will explain. Before I went to see Sal, I started reading my aunt's journal and all she talked about was how wonderful you are, and she was naming you to be Kyle's guardian if I chose to refuse the position and the inheritance. Kyle does nothing but talk about you and how great you are. I can't help it. I was feeling a little insecure about my place here."

Lincoln kept his eyes on her, but never said a thing, causing Maddie to take a step back.

"So, anyway, after I went to Sal's to talk to him, I figured if I was going to leave, I should at least take care of the rest of things in my aunt's closet. In the closet, I found all her old journals. All the way back to the time Kyle was born and before," Maddie stated. More softly, she said, "I found out a lot, Lincoln. My sister was Kyle's birth mother.

At sixteen-years-old she gave birth to Kyle. When she came back, my mother told me my aunt died. In the meantime, my aunt adopted Kyle, which is why they stopped all communication with her. Kyle is my nephew, Lincoln—not my cousin."

Lincoln's face never changed, and Maddie almost wondered if he were listening.

"I decided to stay. Not because Kyle is my blood, but because I realized the moment I found out that I already loved him. I couldn't leave Kyle even if I wanted to. He's grown on me, Lincoln." Lincoln still had not said a word. "Judge me all you want, but you're not in my shoes. You didn't get pulled out of your life to start a new one. I gave up everything to come here. And I'm glad I did. Not only did I gain Kyle in my life, but I've discovered the life I led in Boston wasn't the real me. So, go ahead. Be mad. I just don't care anymore." Turning her back on Lincoln, Maddie started walking toward the house only to have Lincoln gently take her by the arm.

"Maddie, I'm sorry. It's not that I've been judging you. I get it. Your whole life has been turned upside down. I wasn't just worried about Kyle, though. I was worried about me."

Maddie turned and met his eyes. "What?"

"I was worried I'd never see you again. I know, it's selfish, but I didn't want you to go. Have I fallen for you? It seems like it. I honestly don't think I've ever been in love before, but I can tell you this. I don't want you to go. I want you to stay right here, and I will help you with Kyle. And help you with the farm. I want to be helping you do whatever it is that you want to do. Except leave, Maddie. I need you to stay."

Maddie grabbed his arm and pulled him closer. "That depends. You going to leave any more freezers unplugged or gates open?" she teased.

Laughing, Lincoln pulled her tighter against him. "That's only because my mind was on you, instead of the task at hand. You think we can make this work?"

Maddie wrapped her arms around him. "I'm up for it if you are."

"You tell me," he replied as he leaned in and his lips touched hers.

Dear Reader:

I really loved writing *Dandelion Dreams*, the first book in the Cove's Port Series. I quickly discovered how much I loved Cove's Port; it reminds me so much of the small coastal towns here in Maine.

The next book in the series, *Daisies and Sunshine*, will be out at the end of July. Remington "Remi" Peterson left her life in New York to start over in Cove's Port. Buying the old inn sight unseen may not have been the smartest decision—at least not to her ex-husband and son—but it was the right decision. Staying behind was not an option. Not if she wanted to be happy. A failed marriage and empty nest were all that she was leaving behind.

The inn comes with its own problems. Tackling the renovations may just be the hardest thing she's ever done. That is, until she hires the local handyman, Grant Williams. Grant drives her crazy with his penchant for timeliness and being so meticulous about his work. She drives him nuts when she changes things on a whim.

Starting over is just what Remi needs, but can she pull it off and forget about her past?

I hope you enjoy the Cove's Port Series as much as I enjoy writing it. Look for Remi's story, *Daisies and Sunshine*, in July!

Happy Reading!

Penny Harmon

About the Author

Penny Harmon began writing at an early age and developed a great love of words over the years. After her children were grown, she took her writing to the next level and began publishing in both newspapers and magazines. In January of 2016, she published her first novella, *Complicated Inheritance*. Since then, she has published several novels, including her *Rocky Isle Romance Series, Trying to Forget You,* and *Dragonfly Wishes.*

Penny lives in Maine with her long-time partner, Dan, three grandchildren, two dogs, two cats, and fish. She enjoys spending time with all nine of her grandchildren and working on DIY projects, especially those that involve repurposing.

Other Books by Penny Harmon

Complicated Inheritance

Rocky Isle Romance Series:
I Saw Him First
Fallen for the King
Love with Your Everything
The Magic of the Sunrise
Unequivocal Blindness
Bring Me Home: A Rocky Isle Reunion

Trying to Forget You
No Final Destination
Christmas at Moosehead Lake
Dragonfly Wishes

You can follow Penny Harmon at:
https://www.facebook.com/pennyharmonauthor
https://www.twitter.com/PennyH_Author
https://www.pennyharmon.com

www.ingramcontent.com/pod-product-compliance
Lightning Source LLC
Chambersburg PA
CBHW021955120726
47992CB00001B/266